IT WAS
AND
WAS NOT
SO

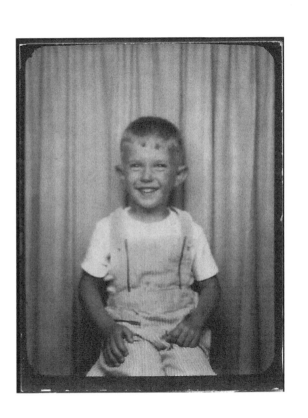

IT WAS
AND
WAS NOT
SO

Bill Castle

Paramount Market Publishing, Inc.

Paramount Market Publishing, Inc.
274 North Goodman Street, STE D-214
Rochester, NY 14607
www.paramountbooks.com
607-275-8100

Publisher: James Madden
Editorial Director: Doris Walsh

Copyright © 2018 William W. Castle
Printed in USA

This is a work of fiction. Names, characters, places and incidents are either the product of the author's imagination or are used fictiously, and any resemblance to actual persons, living or dead, businesses, companies, events or locales is entirely coincidental.

Cataloging in Publication Data available
ISBN-10: 1-941688-56-X | ISBN-13: 978-1-941688-56-4 *paper*
eISBN: 978-1-941688-57-1

For Calabrese and Tiffany

Contents

CHAPTER 1

Now

I AM AN OLD MAN. Old is a simple word that comes to us first in an odd syntax. How old are you? We are prompted the answer. How early can we repeat it? Two? "How," they ask and we give a number, four or seven, or ten. "How" is the question that comes last in our own questioning, after why and when, after where, after who. And then just old. I am old. When did I decide that? At seventy, seventy-five, sixty-five? After thousands and thousands of nows, the question finally makes sense. How? But then there is no answer.

———

old

/ōld/

adjective
having lived for a long time; no longer young.

I taught fifth grade for 47 years at Our Lady of Pompeii, an elementary school in Greenwich Village. I retired at 70 and tutored writing in small groups for five years as part of an after-school program.

I was forgetting. Forgetting words, or do I mean losing words. I felt a gnawing dullness. No, no, not dull, the opposite: alert, more like panic, but not panic, fear maybe, phobia without a category. Fear can alert you, but to what? It's chilly. Make a fire in the fireplace. Put on some water for tea.

Stories never begin at the beginning. I mean real stories in life aren't started with a beginning. They muddle along in the middle and then wind back to a start that makes itself known when you least expect it, an awareness that clings to the truth in ways that can't be shaken.

Oh yes, the panic. It was about the forgetting and it started one night at Ruth's place. Ruth had invited me to dinner, a text message that had said maybe Dorothy would be there, maybe her husband Gordon.

I had taught with Ruth my last eleven years before retiring. We knew each other well. The kind of knowing that has a casualness except when it becomes concern. Ruth had started to be concerned.

"You're such a good cook. This is delicious," I said.

"Yes. You compete with New York's finest restaurants," Gordon said. Gordon's wife Dorothy had taught with us before she became a principal at another school.

"And the twelve dollar bottle of wine doesn't cost forty dollars," Dorothy said.

"Even the . . ." I looked down at my plate. I couldn't name it.

"The High Line was mobbed today," Ruth said. "And I was there early."

"Is it because we're getting old that everything always seems so crowded?" Dorothy said.

I stared at my plate, but I still couldn't name it. I smiled at the plate. The vegetable is, I said in my mind. I ran through the alphabet.

"I'm not getting old," Gordon said. "I decided last month not to. It was a big relief."

Over the laughter I said, "Broccoli."

"What was that, Bill?" Ruth said.

"The broccoli, how did you make it? Only you can make broccoli fancy," I said.

"Good Housekeeping cookbook, 1959. It was my mother's."

"Good old Mama Irene," I said. "I loved her."

"Even when she's dead, she tells me what to do," Ruth said.

After Dorothy and Gordon left, Ruth talked me into another glass of wine and presented the solution to her concern. Ruth always had a solution, even when the problem wasn't really clear.

"I have a student for you," Ruth began. "Johnny Norkus. He's in third grade. He had a much older brother at the school, but that was still probably after you retired. The family had moved here from Lithuania. I remember that. The mother was large, tall and just big, but beautiful."

"Wait, wait, wait." It was hard to stop Ruth. "What do you mean you have a student for me? I don't need a student. I don't want a student."

"Bill, this kid could really get on track with your help. I thought of you as soon as Sister Colleen mentioned the family needed a tutor."

"I don't want a student. Sure I could use the money, this is New York, but."

"But what? You need time to sit home and brood?"

"I am not brooding."

"I'm sorry, that was harsh. It must be hard being alone after all those years."

"I like alone. Dan died almost two years ago. He was eighty-three. People die. We had a lot of great years together."

"Okay, it's not about that. It's that part of teaching, that thing you love, a bright kid that just can't get it."

"I'll hear you out, but I'm not saying yes."

"He was around five when they moved here. No English but he picked it up quickly. They did a year with some kind of Montessori pre-school thing. He came to us in first grade. You know, Pompeii doesn't really have much second language support. He floundered a bit but picked up as he went along. Really strong in math. Reading's a bit of a problem, below grade level and the writing's nowhere."

"Broccoli," I said.

"What?"

"Tonight at dinner, I went to say something about the broccoli and I couldn't think of the word."

"That's no big deal. Everyone's talking. You're listening, something occurs to you. The word doesn't come to mind."

"But it was minutes. It was broccoli."

"It's no big deal."

"It's happened before."

"Not asparagus, I hope."

"I forgot you're missing an empathy gene. I really should get going. When's Bob getting back? That dinner was great."

"Too soon. I mean soon. Friday."

"What's going on?"

"No, it's fine. It's normal. Normalized. What a great word. You'll let me know about Johnny Norkus?"

"I'll think about it." We hugged.

"Listen, if kale goes, you'll call me right away."

"Good night, Ruthie."

Walking in the city has a way of clearing your mind. There is a privacy in the crowds of people. I walked everywhere I went and usually only went where I could walk. It was one of the advantages of Manhattan. It was late, for me, after midnight. The streets were crowded. Ruth lived on Hudson Avenue, near the school. She had taught second grade when she first came, still worked there part time as a reading specialist. I cut down Bleecker, past the school entrance at Leroy Street. North on MacDougal, a diagonal across Washington Square Park, up University. I walked this path from my apartment on 24th Street to work every day. All those years. A fast walk. Automatic, private, clear.

I couldn't stop thinking about losing the word broccoli. Ruth called it no big deal. The good deal, deal me in or deal me out, the big deal. After all my life spent teaching, I am still completely unsure what I mean when I say I am thinking. Is worrying thinking? Was I thinking about forgetting or just worrying? Words gone. Names gone. Memories gone. Up Park Avenue, right on 24th Street, a short block, near Lexington, I'm home. No big deal. But there it was. This thing I'm calling panic had settled in even though I couldn't name it.

The next morning I e-mailed Ruth:

Thanks for the great dinner. Appreciate your thinking of me on the Johnny Norkus tutoring thing but I have to pass. Even when I was tutoring a lot just after retiring, I never did one-on-one. So intimidating for the kid. You might remember I usually did groups of three, individual attention but still that student interaction, less spotlight. I'm going to pass on this one. Thanks though. Talk soon.

That afternoon Ruth answered:

I got you two more students. There's a small room available at Jefferson Library from 3 to 4 so I booked it for Tuesdays and Thursdays. You're going to love these kids. I'll call you tonight. This is good. I really appreciate it.

Ruth is both terrific and impossible. She grew up in the city. There's a city personality. The ones who come here as adults, like me, don't have it, not even after decades. Ruth's version had a gentle push to it, a steady steamroller-like push, sweet, inexorable.

I could use the money. Dan's 401K money had lasted him from early retirement at 62 until he died at 83. We had always kept our money separate. One of the secrets to a lasting relationship. I used the remaining money carefully. I still thought of it as Dan's money. Fixed incomes - I called them broken. The archdiocese pension, social security, inflation, deflated, the air out of an untied balloon. I could use the money. I answered Ruth:

Okay, okay, okay. Talk tonight. Thanks (I think).

This whole tutoring gig didn't exist when I first started teaching. The parents were involved but there wasn't this track record of learning and our parents weren't wealthy. That changed. Tutoring paid more per hour than teaching, so you did it. The pay for teachers at an elementary Catholic school in Greenwich Village was enough to get by if your apartment was rent controlled, if you didn't have children, if you didn't own a car, if you had a partner, if you didn't care much about money things. I got by. It felt comfortable enough. It was comfortable.

The other two students that Ruth had signed up for my little tutoring group were a third grade girl from Saint Anthony's, another parochial school on Sullivan Street, and a fourth grade girl at Our Lady of Pompeii. They were both named Christine. Names went in phases over the years. Although I never missed a day, toward the end of teaching I kept seating charts the whole year pretending they were for the substitute. I sometimes switched to last names when the first name wouldn't come to mind, giving them improvised titles: Doctor Reynolds, Senator Jackson, Officer Marinelli.

I don't know why I was nervous about the first tutoring session. I was glad the room wasn't booked for the hour before and the woman in charge let me in to set up. The Jefferson Library had been built as a courthouse in 1877. The space Ruth had reserved was in the basement which had been holding cells for prisoners on their way to trial. The tiny room had a table and six chairs, no windows. Two fluorescent tubes gave a flat bright dulling light. The wall was lined with coat hooks. I laid out the materials for each student: two sheets of lined paper, a pen, a pencil and the typed lesson sheet. I began to relax. I had talked with parents, sorted out drop-off and pick-up times, decided on a focus of written expression, e-mailed a basic syllabus, received appreciative cursory agreements. Caring parents, glad to have a solution. I went to meet them in the lobby.

"Nothing on the table please. No books, no notebooks, nothing," I said. "Hang your jackets on the hooks and have a seat."

"Johnny, this is Christine and Christine. Christine, meet Johnny and Christine. Christine, meet Christine and Johnny." We all laughed. "I'm Mr. Calvin. Christine, please read the first instruction for today where it says Lesson One."

Christine read. "I like the rain, even when I have to go out in it. But especially when I can watch it from my window."

"Write a few sentences, as many as you want that would follow those sentences. Let's write for ten minutes and then share."

We all wrote. I always wrote when they did, weighing in on how easy or difficult a prompt was. "Let's start with Queen Christine the Third," I said, indicating the third grader from Saint Anthony's.

"Pow, bang, shoop. Watch out for that raindrop. Oh no, it got me."

"Good. Good," I said. "I like shoop. I like raindrops that go shoop. I'll go next," I said. "My newspaper is a soggy, wet mess. The headlines are a blur which might be a lucky break for me," I read. "Excellent Mr. Calvin. Outstanding. Stupendous," I said. They laughed. "Next, Queen Christina the Fourth," I said to the fourth grader.

"I knew the rain was lying to me. Pretending not to be a cold, wet, meany. But I loved its sparkly lie."

"Lovely. Sparkly lies. Nice. Captain Johnny, let's hear it."

"I am dry. The rain is a mud puddle. Don't step in it."

"A great start. A warning, suspense. Let's write more on this for Thursday's assignment." I kept their titles that I had made up that first day for the rest of the year. No one ever mentioned them or showed in any way that this wasn't how every teacher addressed them. "Captain Johnny, pick a letter from the box. It's a D. Let's all write a word that starts with a D."

We all wrote and shared. Double, desk, dangerous. "My word is doubt. Let's write a sentence for each of our four words. Now don't define the word, use it in a sentence. Try to make the sentence show the reader what the word means."

"What's the reader?" Johnny asked.

"The person who reads your sentence."

"We are the writers. Right, Mr. Calvin?"

"Yes. Writing is usually for a reader," I said.

"I sometimes write a secret," Christine said.

"I like that," I said. "Writing a secret. Then there wouldn't be a reader."

"Until you wanted to tell the secret. Then you could let someone read it," the other Christine said.

"Then it wouldn't be a secret anymore," Johnny said.

"Sometimes you can share a secret."

Johnny stared down at the table. His hair stood up in tangled tufts. His school uniform, a silly miniature-man outfit, white shirt and plaid tie, was in clownish disarray. The shirt was wrinkled and hung half-way out of his pants, the tie loosened from the open collar. "Then it wouldn't be a secret," he repeated.

"Let's write," I said. We wrote and shared and I collected the day's writings. "Good work today. You have the additional assignment for Thursday on the lesson sheet. That's it for Lesson One. Only one thousand seven hundred and thirty two lessons to go." The two Christines looked at me skeptically. Johnny smiled.

Walking home, I thought of today's words: double, desk, dangerous, doubt, turning the meanings and the possible contexts in my mind as though it were a secret code I couldn't decipher. "Then it wouldn't be a secret," I said out loud.

It happened to Bill Calvin more frequently in the following days. He would start to say a word and it wouldn't come to mind. It surrounded his sense of old, his sense of being old. With the disappearing words he began to think of his first baby words, of that early love of words that had stayed with him his whole life. His obsession with the single word stemmed from his sense of a word being invented, conjured, named because it split from all the other words available, to hint at something different. Even as a baby he wrestled at words inside himself until their meaning altered what he knew. He picked some as favorites, favoring them in everything he thought or said.

Lost words can haunt you in their absence. Is remembering the opposite of forgetting? Or is forgetting the opposite of learning, of knowing? Perhaps the forgetting accounts for this haunting by his baby-self.

✿

An old man sits by the fire, always the fire. He has propped on a

table pulled to his rocking chair to serve the purpose, a large book,
unwieldy in its size and weight although it is only volume A through
O of the Oxford English Dictionary. Published in 1952 it is already
missing the vocabulary of the technological world he is ignoring. He
uses a magnifying glass to read the tiny print. It takes him minutes to
locate the word he is looking for: paramnesia.

---

paramnesia
/ˌperamˈnēZH(ē)ə/

noun

a distortion of memory in which fact and fantasy are confused.

Is memory words? Of course there are images, places, objects, but try to conjure them and you'll need words. You may see the grape arbor in your mind. Are there grapes? Are they ripe? Perhaps it's winter. Are the wooden struts laden with snow? Already you need the word grape, you need the word arbor. Hold tightly to that memory and a flood of words will come to you or elude you.

There are only months between the time that we can't talk and there is no memory, and the beginning of language and recollection. Bill Calvin's thoughts are stuck in the blankness of those days. He sits by the fire and stares into the flames, into that blankness. As infants we don't make up words. We hear the words of the people around us and repeat them; store them in context, in understanding or confusion.

The old man sits by the fire. There is a story to tell, a fiction, perhaps
the old once upon a time, at least a once, for certain a time.

It's a strange process this losing or forgetting words. It's never the ones that seem logical. Not augmented, belligerent, cavalier, denigrated, efficacy, on through the alphabet, umbilical, veracity, winsome. Those words are still there for Bill Calvin, odd and random.

---

quotidian
/kwō'tidēən/

adjective
of or occurring every day; daily.

He doesn't lose the word quotidian, but the words it refers to. The ones he reaches for and stalls until he can find a substitute, or pretend a changed idea, or admit a lost train of thought. It's odd that often the meanings are still there, that he can still think through these ideas that a single word has encapsulated, verisimilitude, or visceral or empathetic. Words are our ideas and our memories. His alarm at losing them is justified. There is something that he is trying to remember. A memory perhaps that he never had that he needs to conjure for the first time.

The old man stares into the fire. He will have to depend on the omniscient lies of this fiction to parse out the few available truths. He struggles to give rein to every first person singular of his past; to the baby, the toddler and the little boy. The baby, the toddler, the boy; they are him, yes, but strangers too. He stares at photographs with no connection, no memory, no empathy.

Daily, simple nouns disappear before he can articulate them. Sometimes with the object in his vision. It primes the pumping of panic and leaves him with a determination to mend this rent in the very fabric of his consciousness. As he stares into the fire, it separates his logical contentment from an inexorable sadness.

He grapples for the words to say what he means. He suspects that this start, this inclination to start is before words or that it rests at the very start of language. He can't comprehend this need to explain something, but it has settled like aging into his bones.

This something vaguely connects to an overwhelming unease morphing into panic. It stops his breath with its blackness, blankness, bottomlessness.

The old man sits by the fire. There is a chill. He invites you to take the comfortable chair, closest to the blazing logs. The sparks bounce off the fine-meshed screen. He takes a grey throw and covers your lap. "A story is the words between the remembering," he says. "It is the connections we invent to make it comprehensible." He sits back down in the rocker and begins.

His story begins like yours, as a baby's story. He tries as much as possible to let the baby tell it, to not interrupt. Like all stories it is told with words, but this story is also about words. It balances precariously between the very earliest baby words and this losing of words, this forgetting, that he is experiencing as an old man. And so the story: the baby's story, the boy's story, the man's, the old man's; their constantly changing I mixed with the omniscient possibilities.

It starts: "The first confusion stayed and stayed." No, no. He must let the baby tell it. He must try to not interrupt.

CHAPTER 2

Shoo Shoo Baby

baby

/ˈbābē/

noun

a very young child, especially one newly or recently born.

I WAS THE BABY of the family, the first boy after six girls counting the one before me that died at birth. We all were separated in nearly two-year increments. Lena, the next youngest, was five years old when I was born and the oldest Joanne was fifteen. The earliest word I remember is baby. It was my name in those baby years. It is the memory that starts the remembering. Perhaps the memory that starts the confusion. I was born into a world of girls and women. My father was a photograph, tall and solemn in his army uniform. There is actually no memory of that photo, though I can see it now hanging in my hallway. I've been told it hung in the living room of the old Victorian where we lived in those early years. As I try to remember, I come first to words and then much later to images of places, things and people.

Baby Face. You've got the cutest little baby face. Be my, be my baby. Walking my baby . . . My baby just cares for me. Shoo Shoo Baby. Words with the lilt of music still stay in my mind. I was the baby. And baby was the cutest, the sweetest, the shoo shoo shooest. Only with the word "the" did my baby title lose its adoration. "Where's the baby?" "Get the baby." "The baby can't have that." With the word "the" my title took on a slight, confusing alarm.

By my third summer I would have been two and a half, words were the greatest source of my delight. Words spoken and sung and constantly, beggingly read to me. My sister Joanne, who turned seventeen that summer, and Carolyn, already fifteen, became my other mothers. But even the younger girls, Maria, Eleanor and Lena, played mothering as a favorite game and I was the baby doll – *Shoo Shoo Baby*.

I never spoke in partial phonemes, in hinted syllables of the words I heard. No wawa or dada. I waited in silence until I mastered the whole connected word. I figured out a syntax that put together those words more or less the way others did. I had plenty of chances to hear that way in the household chatter of my sisters. It came at me in circular motion, in high pitched tones that imitated laughter or giggles and sometimes was laughing and giggling.

The summers with no school extended that cacophony of words. Although I loved words from the start, I harbored them in a determined silence. The quiet baby. The good baby.

"He never cried," Bonnie, my mother, would say as the beginning of a retold anecdote long into my adulthood.

I loved the lyrics of the songs my sisters played constantly, but they surfaced in the muddle of all the household sounds. My favorite words were in the stories and poems that were read to me, clear and repeated, in the same exact order during the quiet before bedtime.

The words I spoke were coaxed out of me, although I practiced speaking words in my alone time. My sisters paraded this ability to speak clearly and precisely, especially my identification of each of them, spoken without any shortening. No nicknames. "Lena, Eleanor, Maria, Carolyn, Joanne." My mother was "Mom." The photo on the wall was "Dad," even though my sisters used the diminutive, mommy and daddy just as often. If prompted to say my mother's name, Bonnie, I would giggle and refuse.

"Who is this? Her name's Bonnie?"

"Mom," I would say.

All the stories and poems were in two volumes of a book called *The Junior Instructor*. There must have been years of hearing the rhymes and poems and stories but in that summer of 1945 my favorites were 'The Gingerbread Man,' 'The Little Kitten Who Forgot Kitten Talk,' and 'The Teeny-Tiny Woman'. My sisters and mother took turns reading so the repetition of my favorites generally wasn't an issue, except for 'The Teeny-Tiny Woman' which would always elicit some resistance that required coaxing. Only Maria loved reading it. She used a high pitched voice and a rapid fire delivery.

"There was once upon a time," it began. I played this phrase in my mind again and again, but I did not understand this notion of time that was not an hour or a week, a day or a year.

> *There was once upon a time a teeny-tiny*
> *woman who lived in a teeny-tiny house in a*
> *teeny-tiny village. Now, one day this*
> *teeny-tiny woman put on her teeny-tiny bonnet*
> *and went out of her teeny-tiny house to take a*
> *teeny-tiny walk.*

The teeny-tiny adjectives went on and on in this story and could reduce me to uncontrollable giggles that sometimes ended in uncontrollable hiccups.

My mother would call up the steps, "It's supposed to be a bedtime story. As in bed. As in sleep."

Just when the two or three stories were about to finish and the light turned off I would say, "Poetry, please?" It was this clearly enunciated request that always worked, at least for one poem. Probably because the rhythm of these words usually lulled me to sleep before the light was turned out in my tiny room at the end of the hall.

And so my carefully pronounced words countered any possible concern over my silence. The large fenced-in yard allowed alone time. The grape arbor or the outdoor pump or the oak tree were separate countries in my baby world. This recluse was a relief from the whirlwind world of my sisters. My earliest remembered images are the private worlds I created at the bottom of the grassy hill, behind the stalks of corn in the vegetable garden, and under the huge rosebush by the side of the house, where words could be practiced, turned over and over again in my mind, their mystery parsed. "Run, run as fast as you can. You can't catch me, I'm the gingerbread man." Once upon a time. Upon a time. Or maybe up on a time.

---

dead
/ded/

adjective
no longer alive.

Dead was a blunt word that held a strange mystery. Julie was dead. My sister who wasn't there. And where was she? Dead. That's where she was. She was just a baby when she got dead and disappeared, like magic but a sad magic.

The girl who had died at five days old due to a malformed heart ignited this early confusion. Dead is such a long time. It stretches away from alive to a tautness that finally approaches the breaking point. It is that breaking point the living need, the separation from the terrible longing that dead hangs on your heart.

While my older sisters ranged in age in those equal increments there was a double increment, a gap between me and Lena because Julie was dead. This gap left more caution for baby, more babying of baby, more confusion for baby.

And so began an impulse to wrestle away from the babyness in spite of its cutest little shoo shoo singing rhythms. The gap held the danger of dead. A gap of disappearing. A sad magic.

That summer had a special event that added to the mystery of dead. I walked with all my sisters and my mom to the small wooden church near our house. We sometimes went to this church but we had a Catholic

God and this God was Methodist. So we went to visit the Methodist God only if it snowed or we were late for the Catholic God because it was just a short walk.

"God is God," my mother always said.

But this event wasn't to visit God. It was held outside where we stood around a big glass case with names printed inside. It was a proud event where two ladies each received a flag gift for being a mother and a gold star.

If I got a gold star, it was stuck to my forehead because I was very good. But these ladies didn't have a gold star on their forehead. The names in the big glass case were honor dead. *Dead.* An old man played a horn and the ladies were given their gifts which made them cry. Carolyn and Mom cried and my mom hugged Lena because she started to cry too. Mrs. Ruccio, who lived across the road but down the hill, was one of the ladies and my mom and Joanne went up and hugged her because she was now a gold star lady.

I didn't know how Mrs. Ruccio and the other lady had been very good, and I didn't know why the horn music made so many people cry or why this dead was honor. But I did know that dead was a long, long time.

So dead became a secret mystery for me. In my silence I seldom questioned and there was a feeling around the word dead that wasn't around words I did question like airplane or water pump or radio. The mystery of dead was my first confusion and it began to be buried inside my secret fears.

But in the musical, giggling chaos of the world my mom and sisters created, I seldom turned these things in my mind.

My first real memories blossomed that third summer and from that point I recall the slowly changing seasons. The light to dark, the waning heat, the colors of fall filled me with wonder as that third summer changed to autumn.

This change meant back to school for my sisters which was its own wonder. Mornings burst into action while it was still dark. They were louder and more urgent than summer mornings. Everyone was up at once and I was up too so I wouldn't miss any of the excitement. These mornings combine, as I recall them, into repeated patterns. There was the constant planning: clothes selected and laid out carefully, hair wrapped and pinned very funny and baths taken the night before. In spite of all of this, the morning brought an urgent dizziness of things lost and things found. Juggling for more time in the bathroom and just one minute of time to do just one thing in the bathroom mirror.

I couldn't understand but clothes might be wrong. So wrong that Mom would help find different ones before there were tears.

---

borrow
/ˈbärō, ˈbôrō/

verb
take and use something that belongs to someone else with the intention of returning it.

Borrowing was a word with rules. And although I hoped to someday borrow like my sisters, I had to figure out these rules first because there were often borrowing arguments which were bad. I knew you had to be careful with borrowed things which belonged to another person. And you had to give them back because they weren't a present and you had to clearly agree when you would borrow and which thing and maybe which color.

"No borrowing," my mother shouted one morning.

"Mommy," Maria whined.

"It's only Eleanor, she's the problem," Carolyn said.

"That's not true," Eleanor said. "I thought the blue scarf was Joanne's and she said I could . . ." and then she began to cry.

No borrowing was the rule for several weeks. When they could borrow again, my sisters seldom argued over the rules. But I never borrowed, although I wanted to.

grades
/grād/

noun

a particular level of rank, quality, proficiency, intensity, or value.

My sisters were in grades and they got grades. They got good grades and might cry if they got a bad grade. Lena was already in third grade. And her skirts were too short so she wore some of Eleanor's while Mom sewed two new ones. Eleanor was in the fifth grade and her teacher, Mrs. Dawson, was the nicest in the whole school. Maria went on the second bus this year because she was in the seventh grade. Maria was a beauty or maybe was going to be a beauty. Joanne said so and Carolyn told a joke about Maria breaking boys' hearts and everyone laughed, but not Maria. And I didn't laugh because I knew you had to be careful and not break things. Carolyn stopped being in a number and was just a freshmen, and best of all Joanne was a junior and might go to the junior prom which was a long time away but still excited her.

The crazy mornings had a waking start and a definite finish because the two buses would arrive on the road outside our house one after the other. Sometimes there was time for kisses to my mother and sometimes to me. But usually mine were thrown to me and I learned to throw one too, kissing my hand and pushing the kiss into the air. My mom and I would stand on the porch and sometimes Mom would lift me up to the railing so I could wave and then the house was quiet.

The quiet held a contentment, almost a relief. My mother's days were filled with chores; laundry, sewing, cleaning and cooking. All I had to do was be good. Behave, which included being careful.

"He's so good. He never cries." I had already overheard my mother say this more than once. "I mean, he won't turn three until January," she would say proudly. "He'll scrunch up his face if he falls. And if I tell him no, sometimes he'll let out a coaxing, whistling, drawn out 'oh' which I know I shouldn't, but I usually give into, but he's so good."

So I became determined not to cry. To be the good baby, sweet baby,

Shoo-Shoo Baby. Mom called me Baby Doll, my Baby Doll.

I always chose to be outside. There weren't many rules. I knew not to climb the white wooden fence with heavy logs connecting the poles. Not even to sit on it like my sisters did. I knew to answer when she called out "Baby Doll" or "What are you up to?"

"Here" was enough to satisfy her. I could pull down the pump handle to make water come out of the spout, but not too much. I could eat the grapes when they weren't green, but not too much. I was good. I knew how to be good which was just like behaving. And if I was good, I was left alone.

I loved alone. I still wore the baby's cloak of invisibility under a blanket or behind the sofa, but my favorite alone was my secret places outdoors, in the cornstalks, behind the oak tree and especially under the rose bush.

The huge sprawling bush bloomed with bright red flowers from early spring until the first frost. There was a wide sinking of the ground on one side that allowed me to crawl into what seemed like a large cave with the smell of dirt and flowers. You had to be careful of the thorns and I dug this entrance deeper with my shovel so I could easily crawl in or out. The only toys I took into this place were a bucket that was blue with a beach and an ocean and sand painted on the side, and a blue shovel. I had never seen an ocean or a beach and what Joanne said was sand looked like brown dirt. My bucket and shovel were my favorite things. With them I hollowed out the dirt beneath the rose bush and built a world with mountains and valleys, roads and bridges. Sticks from under the oak tree and rocks from the bottom of the hill created fences and houses and towns. Dirty was never not behaving.

"My dirty Baby Doll," my mother would laugh. "Take off your shoes and march up to the bathroom."

Once when I made a lake with water from the pump, I was not behaved. Mud, my mother called it, which was wet dirt. I was washed off under the pump which Eleanor said I liked too much and no mud became a new rule.

I had tiny soldiers, nine of them, like the boy who was sick and lay in bed in one of my poems, *The Land of Counterpane*:

> *And sometimes for an hour or so*
> *I watched my leaden soldiers go,*
> *With different uniforms and drills,*
> *Among the bed-clothes, through the hills;*

But I seldom played with my tiny soldiers. I didn't want to make a war. Like my sisters, I wanted the real war to be over. I wasn't really sure how a war worked or even what it was. So I never brought my soldiers to my rosebush secret place. Or even made stick people like I did under the oak tree. This secret land had no soldiers, no war, no people, just me. Much of my time here was spent practicing words and songs and poems and figuring out words and conversations I had heard. I found that music words were in my head, but I only tested this out under the rose bush. I would sing about *Walking My Baby Back Home*, repeating the same part over and over.

But I stayed silent when my sisters would sing and dance to the radio playing that song, or when everyone gathered around the player piano and sang all the verses as my sisters took turns pumping the pedals to make the music keys work and the words roll by. I laughed and clapped and even danced, but I didn't sing except in my secret place.

"I will be going outside now," I would announce to my mother and she would laugh her approval.

I ran everywhere I went in the world of our backyard. I'm told I walked late. But almost from the start, running was more interesting than walking. I'd run to the arbor to get some grapes and run down to the oak tree to eat them. I would run down the hill to the bottom fence, get as many stones as I could carry then run up the hill to the rosebush. *Run, run as fast as you can. You can't catch me I'm the Gingerbread Man.*

One of my favorite games was to roll down the hill like a log, and then run to the top as fast as I could and then fall to the ground and roll like a log and then dizzily struggle to the top of the hill as many times as I could until, exhausted, I collapsed somewhere in the middle and the clouds seemed to spin and the sweet, sour smell of the new mown grass filled my breathing until my belly felt funny and I would close my eyes tight and feel the world inside me spin, a feeling of glee, a feeling of freedom.

But it was one time, lying on that hill that I first felt my glee interrupted by a fear that I could not understand. A fear of disappearing like Julie or the honor dead. The squinting dizziness had centered a special me into the sun and the spinning clouds. And knowing that me started a confusing fear which I shook away by rolling back to the bottom of the hill so fast that I hit the fence with a force and almost cried, not for the hurt from the fence but for something else. For something else.

I can't explain this early inclination to run, when walking had come late. I don't know why talking, so elaborately practiced and skilled, still held a preference for silence.

When I was invisible inside my secret place, I tried to sort out these confusions, but then I would change to practicing songs or poems or words.

----

perhaps
/pər'(h)aps/

adverb
used to express uncertainty or possibility.

"Perhaps," I would say carefully pronouncing each syllable. Perhaps was a fine word. It told that maybe you would but it was not like a promise. Perhaps could be a word alone like yes or no and so I liked it. Perhaps could be the answer to a lot of questions and I especially liked it because it always made my sisters laugh.

I was overheard only once practicing out loud. It might have been that same autumn. Maria was sitting on the fence outside the house and heard me saying in a loud voice:

I have a little shadow that goes in and out with me,
And what can be the use of him is more than I can see.
He is very, very like me from the heels up to the head;
And I see him jump before me, when I jump into my bed.
The funniest thing about him is the way he likes to grow-
Not at all like proper children, which is always very slow.

Maria ran into the house and told everyone. As the story was retold in the passing years, it was exaggerated into my reciting the entire poem and made me even younger than I was.

"I don't even think he was two," someone would say. "Word-for-word without a pause, all the verses."

I remember that evening, after Maria had overheard me, Mom and Joanne and Carolyn asked me please to say the poem, just some of it. But I remained silent.

Carolyn even said "Pretty please, with sugar on top." Which made me laugh but I refused.

My silence was polite. "No thank you," I might say. Or, "Thank you, I'd rather not."

Finally my mother hugged me and said, "You'll say it for us another day."

"Perhaps," I said.

And so there was no baby talk for baby and words were harbored in silence as secret wondrous things to be practiced in secret places and used to solve some mystery or other that sorted out my baby world and separated my glee from a halting confusion and a confusing sadness.

CHAPTER 3

When Daddy Comes Marching
Home Again Hurrah, Hurrah

I WAS BORN on the perihelion, a fact I only learned as an old man. It's the day when the Earth, in its ellipse, is closest to the sun. It occurs in early January and varies from year to year as much as seventy-two hours. In the northern hemisphere it is always cold and sometimes snowy and sunless, clouds blocking the closest view of our closest star as we speed past it.

January 2, 1946 was not the perihelion but it was frigid cold and snowy. It is my first birthday memory, when I turned three.

Event memories that happen each year and daily memories that form patterns – changing seasons, falling leaves and snow and blossoms, collapse into a single recollection, evolve into photographs' lies and stories that edit out realities for punch lines, or perhaps to protect the happy times, the happy birthdays, the happy childhood.

It isn't that memory starts with language, but language allows a way of coming to memory. And so I cling to the earliest words that turned in my baby mind to unravel my story from the stories.

This first birthday memory is not of balloons or cake and candles or presents. Although there are photographs, proof that there was a cake with candles and a present and a funny cone hat that I had to wear but did not find funny.

I recall that on this birthday my mother presented to us a large calendar with much fanfare and excitement. Above each printed calendar number, starting on the second of January, she had made circled red numbers counting backwards from the number thirty-five.

Joanne took a nail and pounded it into the wall above our kitchen table, and Carolyn hung the calendar by a tiny ring and everyone clapped so I clapped too.

And why did Mom turn our calendar into backward days? Because when the number reached zero, Dad, Daddy, Ray, the tall uniformed man in the photo on the living room wall, would be home. Home for good.

"For good?" Maria kept asking. She remembered the last time, when only after days home, Daddy had left again and was shipped out. Joanne and Carolyn remembered, too, and they liked this "for good" assurance.

I knew what a ship was. I had a picture of a ship in my bedroom. But I didn't know how you could be shipped, or why this shipping would be out. But none of that mattered now because this home was for good and good was always good and never bad.

The war had already been over a long time. Long before my birthday, before snow came and Jesus' Christmas with Santa Claus, even before the leaves turned orange and red and fell to the ground.

The radio told us that the war was over on a hot August morning. My mom cried uncontrollably, assuring us between sobs that everything was alright.

"Happy tears," she would say. "It's over, the war is over. Happy tears."

The radio was usually songs and I could not understand the talking that brought everyone to a focused quiet. In the months before the war ended everyone would gather around the radio in the early evening before dinner. This was news but not new. The man on the radio would explain about the war. I knew it was the second one, all over the world, but not here so Dad had to go where it was. Over there, like in the song.

I didn't understand the explaining. Carolyn might put her finger to her lips if anyone talked which meant stay quiet. But usually no one spoke anyhow, except for Mom or Joanne who might say, "No, Daddy is not there." or "Daddy would be fine."

When the news was done and the radio would be songs again, the quiet slowly ebbed into the noisy talking.

That evening, after the radio told us the war was over, we had a dinner that Mom said was special and then she surprised us with a chocolate cake she had baked. Songs on the player piano were pumped out and sung. Lena and Maria were allowed to roll up the smaller rug by the piano and my sisters danced and my mom held me and danced.

Eleanor played one of the songs she could make by pressing the keys and everyone sang, *Over There, Over There.*

But it wasn't until the next day sitting in the middle of the drying cornstalks that I sang. I mimicked the tune to the funny rhymes.

> *Hoist the flag and let her fly*
> *Yankee Doodle do or die*
> *Pack your little kit*
> *Show your grit, do your bit.*

And I sang the final lines again and again in my loudest baby voice.

> *And we won't come back till it's over, over there.*
> *And we won't come back till it's over, over there.*

Later, after my sisters had started back to school, the radio man explained the war was now officially over.

---

officially
/ə ˈfiSHəlē/

adverb
in a formal and public way.

Officially became a new favorite word. If asked what I wanted for breakfast I might say, "Officially, Cheerios."

As the days slowly passed in my baby time, I somehow formed an idea of future out of repeated nows, out of Santa coming for Jesus' Christmas, and a new year with a new number before my birthday. And especially in the backward counting days until he, Dad, Daddy, Ray, would be home for good.

Christmas memories are a blank in those early years. My first Christmas memory, before I turned three, is of my favorite new songs called carols, but not Carolyn like my sister, and the Christmas stories and poems that I begged to hear again and again. But even this memory combines with other Christmases and first snows into an invented day that happens in any year or every year. The recollection of the first snow of winter whenever it came is a feeling of awe, a sense of the best kind of magic, both unexpected and wonderful. Even now as an old man those first snowflakes in any given winter can create that feeling.

I had full-body, zippering, pulling, itching, wool, warm clothes for those frigid, snowy days. I even had clothes for my hands. My first sled was a piece of cardboard and the big yard with the steep, grassy hill gave a thrilling ride to the bottom with such speed that the bank of snow against the fence stopped your ride with a sudden jolt. I would run to the top of the hill and repeat the ride and run again to the top and jump onto the cardboard, without stopping, barely balancing on the square of cardboard or rolling off, and lying on the hill listening to my panting breath.

There is a photo that pretends a memory of that third Christmas. It is an artifact that tries to prompt the recollection of a self in a forgotten time. I am sitting under a fat, bushy tree decorated with lights and garlands of popcorn and cranberries. I am centered on a round, plastic dish sled. I see it as red though the photo is black and white. I am tightly gripping the plastic handles.

I don't know if there was snow my third Christmas, but in my memory there was the best, most beautiful snowfall. I do recall many snow years with that sled. My cardboard sleds didn't have handles which were the best part of this new sled. It moved with an amazing speed. If I leaned in one direction, I could slightly guide the sled and even turn at the end of the hill to slow down before I hit the snow bank by the fence.

I remember that the best part of Christmas was the weeks before with the season's stories and songs whose words I learned more quickly and stored in my mind to hear in my silent singing anytime I wanted.

"*Away in a manger, no crib for a bed,*" I might hear inside my head when the lights were off and I was warm under the quilt of patches, blue and orange, and green and striped and plaid. My favorite warm, deep inside me in my own thoughts, "*no crib for a bed.*" But also in my bed, I might speak softly my new favorite poems or stories during those holiday weeks.

"*When out on the roof, I heard such a clatter, I sprang to the window to see what was the matter,*" I would say out loud. And then I might listen carefully to hear such a clatter on my own roof until I fell into a deep baby sleep.

The next day, after my birthday, my mother held me up so I could mark the first X over the number 2 and the red circled number 35. And now it was only 34 days until Dad would be home.

I have no memory of my father at this point. The only image is the military photo in our living room. I can't create a possible timeline of when he might have seen me, but from fragmented stories, I think he was already gone for my birth, but saw me once as an infant. This homecoming only loomed large in my mind because my mother and sisters gave it so much talk.

Some words of their talk linked to the confusion of dead. I figured out that if it was honor dead it could only happen in a war when you were killed which was just another kind of dead. But then there was killing, shooting, bombing – confusing kinds of making dead, which my mother made my sisters stop asking about if I seemed to be listening, but mostly if Lena or Maria asked too many questions. Alone I turned these dead ways in my mind and was glad, too, like Carolyn, that my dad was safe and sound. I did not know how you could be sound, but my rules for being good had many things about not safe, which was the baddest you could be.

This story rests in the cradle of these confusions. I have to struggle through the blanks, the forgotten moments and the suppressed fears.

Ready or not, here I come. Things were busy getting ready as the numbers were slowly X'd out. Curtains were taken off the windows and washed and ironed and put back up after the glass was shiny.

When my sisters were home from school, they helped. One sunny Saturday morning, the rugs were hung over the ropes in the backyard, and I helped to hit them with a special loopy-wired stick so dust would fly into the chilling wind and everyone laughed.

Joanne, Carolyn, and Maria painted our kitchen table and cupboards a shiny white, even though they were already white. Lena pestered to help and got to paint some with the big brush, but I was too little. I was often too little to do something and was sometimes too big but I didn't know when I had gotten littler or bigger.

The best getting ready in those counting backward days was when a man came and rolled out a new floor in the kitchen with huge white blocks and little red blocks and black blocks in the middle. My mom knew the man who asked about Ray who was Dad. The man said that he had only been home a month and when he talked about the war my mother told me to go out and play.

---

tomorrow

/tə'môrō/

adverb
on the day after today.

noun
the day after today.

I got to make the final X on the kitchen calendar and the day of Dad home for good was now a tomorrow. Tomorrow was when you woke the next morning. It was a Thursday and all of my sisters were allowed to stay home from school but nobody was sick.

There are too many stories about that day to sort out what I really recall. I know I went to my secret place behind the sofa where I could watch the front door. I remember he was the tallest person I had ever seen and his talk was loud. He wore a brightly colored shirt instead of his uniform like in the photo. My sisters cried those happy tears and hugged and laughed and my mother kissed him a big kiss and my sisters clapped for this.

"Where's the little man?" Dad asked.

"Hey Baby Doll, don't you want to come and give Daddy a big welcome home hug?"

"Baby Doll? Really Bonnie?" He leaned over the sofa into my secret place and shouted: "Where's my welcome?" I stared up at his grin. I liked this grin, but I did not move or answer.

"Come on, hit the road Jack," he yelled.

"Hey Shoo Shoo Baby," Joanne said and lifted me from my secret place, carrying me in her arms to Dad.

"Let's see how tall you got, Jack." Joanne put me down.

"Why do you call him Jack?" Lena asked. "His name's Billy."

It can not be that I didn't know my name but I never thought of the me I was as Billy. My father crouched down to Lena and kissed her on the forehead. "Don't be silly, I know it's Billy. It's just my way, Daisy Mae."

I liked this rhyming dad. Eleanor whispered in my ear about my reminder. I clicked my feet together and stood as tall as I could and did my practiced salute. "Welcome home Sergeant Calvin," I said.

"At ease private." He picked me up and extended his arms so I was high in the air.

"Ray, be careful," my mother said.

He put me down. "Let's go Jack, Daisy Mae, Bonnie, all my lovelies. I got a surprise."

We all followed him through the kitchen and out the back door. There are lots of stories about this surprise which was a sleek, black 1946 Buick convertible. But I have two real memories. One is my father demonstrating how the roof could be rolled back and then lifting me up to see inside. "But top down will have to wait awhile," he said, "'cause it's too chilly Billy."

The other memory is a sensing that my mother did not like this surprise.

"Can we afford this, Ray?" she asked. Later she said, "How can we all fit?"

"Well Daisy Mae will just have to stay home," he said, kissing Joanne on the forehead. Then, "No no, I meant Daisy Mae stays home." He kissed Carolyn. "No wait, Daisy Mae, you'll have to stay home," he said to Eleanor. He went to each of my sisters, calling each of them Daisy Mae and kissing their forehead or hand in consolation for being left behind until everyone was giggling and piling into the car. But my mother did not laugh although she held a frozen smile as she took me onto her lap in the front seat.

That night there was another special dinner and a cake and ice cream on top. After dinner, this tall, grinning, rhyming stranger had another surprise. But I guess it was just a surprise to me. Instead of the paper roll pumping out the songs, he could push the keys and make the music, just like Eleanor could, but lots of songs, smooth and wonderful. And when he sang, he sang like a radio man. He sang *I'll Never Smile Again* and *I'll Get By*. He said "Any requests?" and Maria asked for *Swinging on a Star* which was one of my favorite radio songs. After he sang *I'll Be Seeing You* for Mom, I shouted "*Walking My Baby Back Home.*" Everyone looked at me.

"It's *Walking My Baby Back Home*," he announced. "For the man in the front row. Everybody sing." And I sang, too.

When I had to go to bed I wanted Dad to read to me, but he said, "I ain't such a good reader Jack." Carolyn said she'd read to me.

When I began to get sleepy, Carolyn kissed me goodnight and pulled the quilt up to my chin. Alone in the dark and warmth of my bed I said aloud: "The man in the front row. The man in the front row."

It was in those first weeks and months after my father's return that I became aware of how beautiful my mother was. Her hair was the color of coal, coal-shiny and coal-sleek. And her dark eyes seemed darker because of her light skin. They would go out in the evening without us sometimes. Then her lips would be red and her cheeks a pale pink. When she would come down the staircase into our living room, my father would whistle and my sisters would surround her. Maria said she looked like a movie star. I had never seen a movie, but I knew what Maria meant about the star – shiny and beautiful in the darkest night. Although I still called her Mom, I began to think of her as Bonnie in those days, and then Bonnie Mom. She laughed and mocked this attention on those going-out nights, but I could tell she liked it. She would twirl around so the skirt of her sparkly dress, the color of her hair, would look like it was caught in a wind. My father might take her hand and do what Joanne called 'cool moves,' humming *In The Mood* and turning and tapping. We all laughed and clapped. I had never seen my Bonnie Mom this kind of happy, this star beautiful and maybe like a movie.

But then there was worry. Mom would tell that she was worried and Dad would say she worried too much. I knew right away this worry was an unhappy thing and my dad did not like my mother doing it. Sometimes he even said a swear, which I never did. He would say she worried too damn much and that Mom rained on his parade. I didn't know how a person could rain or even how one person could be a whole parade.

———————

worry
/ˈwər-ē/

verb
give way to anxiety or unease; allow one's mind to dwell on difficulty or troubles.

One surprise that all my sisters said was the very best, was a phonograph player that played songs like the radio man but the exact one that you requested because the song was on a large black plate. I have a real memory of my sisters forming a circle around me, joining hands and singing along with one of the songs we heard all the time on the radio. Carolyn said our record was number one and was the same sisters singing from the radio, the Andrews Sisters. I still can recall this image of my sisters, dancing around me and singing the part that repeated: *Shoo Shoo Shoo Baby*. One of the names they called me. *Shoo Shoo Shoo Baby*.

But my mother worried about the bill for this favorite surprise. She didn't laugh when Dad rhymed loudly over her worry.

"It's not lay-away.

It's play as you pay.

You use it today."

And later in the kitchen, while my sisters danced, my mother's worry rained again on this surprise.

"You always do that," he yelled. And this scared me some because his loud voice was even louder and because of the swear. "Damn it, Bonnie, you always have to rain on my parade."

I knew my dad had gotten his old job back at Irwin Provision Company which was why he was gone most days. I knew that he was gone some nights because he played a piano and sang at a place in the next town, which wasn't a job because he only got a drink if he was thirsty and didn't get money, which was one of the worries.

One time in the middle of the night, I woke up because it was loud and I came downstairs.

"Baby Doll, what are you doing up?" my mother asked me.

"What's up?" my father asked.

I couldn't answer either question so I just shrugged my shoulders which means I don't know.

"I sang your favorite song tonight, Jack" my dad said. Whistling the tune of *Walking My Baby Back Home* he picked me up and began doing some of his cool moves with me in his arms. I had never heard my Mom so loud.

"Ray," she yelled. And I had never heard her say a swear.

"Damn it, put him down." She grabbed me from his arms and his cool moves turned into a stumble. He banged into the small table knocking the new phonograph player to the ground and stumbling again, fell to the floor.

Some of my sisters started down the stairs but my mother said: "Back to bed." And they turned around in the middle without a word.

My father stayed sprawled on the floor and said softly, "Jesus, Bonnie." And then again, "Jesus, Bonnie."

My mother, still holding me, explained as we looked down at my dad, "Your father's drunk." She carried me up to my room, leaving my dad who had rolled over and buried his head in his arms on the living room floor.

In my room she read to me "*The Teeny-Tiny Woman*" without my even asking and kissed me good night. In the dark I said aloud: "Jesus Bonnie." But I had no idea what that meant.

The next day when I got up my father was sitting in the old rocker smoking cigarettes. The phonograph, back on its stand, was playing "*I'll Be Seeing You,*" Mom's favorite song. That whole day and the next, the house was very quiet. But not nice and quiet, like Joanne sometimes mentioned. Not nice.

When we turned the page of the big calendar in the kitchen and the backward counting days were gone completely, I began to think of the future as the slowly melting snow. The no mud rule was harder to obey because my favorite places had turned into wet dirt. I had no name for the huge flowers that began to bloom along the border of our house and the fence at the bottom of our yard, but I loved them. I now know that they are peonies. Their fragrance even now can bring into focus some memory of that time.

By the time the dark green leaves and red roses had bloomed on the huge bush that formed my favorite hiding place, winter was gone and this was spring. Next was summer. And next was fall. In my mind I had the calendar picture of these season names. But I have a true recollection of forming the notion of next in the changing light that became my fourth summer.

next
/nekst/

adjective
of a time or season coming immediately after the time of writing or speaking.

after
/ˈaftər/

preposition
following, subsequent to, at the close/end of.

First there was next, and then there was after. Dad home for good had altered our world completely. After my father's drunk was told. After my dad had sprawled his tallest arms and legs across the rug. After I, in my mother's arms looked down, seeing him stretched out so long, I began calling him Daddy. Daddy made him smaller, and somehow I knew I needed this rhyming singing Daddy Ray to be not so big. Not so giant.

As the days warmed, I dug a deeper bowl in the cavern of my rose bush. I created my mountains and valleys in more detail and inhabited the land with houses intricately layered using sticks and pebbles. But no people, just me. And here I would sit thinking. And in my baby way that thinking became a worry. And because I did not understand, I worried about worry. I wondered why Bonnie Mom worried too damn much, although I did not connect this flickering feeling of unease with my new word.

It was during that time that my father changed my baby name word to babying. Immediately I felt 'no' to my old baby name.

Maybe he said, "You baby him too much."

"Stop babying him," I heard him yell.

And the yell lodged in my no. And so I wrestled at every turn to rid myself of my baby title, of my babyness. Now it held no shoo shoo cuteness. Not even a careful effort to be the good baby was good anymore. My sisters began to call me Billy, perhaps to please my father.

My mother tried but still sometimes slipped and called me Baby Doll.

There was a song that questioned a charming Billy that my sisters would sing. I did not understand it and I did not like it. It repeated "Billy Boy, Billy Boy" and Maria began using this Billy Boy as my name and my other sisters picked it up too.

> *Oh, where have you been*
> *Billy Boy, Billy Boy?*
> *Oh, where have you been,*
> *Charming Billy?*

There is a true memory. The thick blooms of roses perfume the air. The red is bright against the fresh dark green of the leaves that cover the entrance secreting my secret place. I climb in carefully to avoid the thorns. I crawl into the basin which is so deep now that it almost forms walls making me truly invisible even as my baby idea of invisibility was fading.

> *Oh, where have you gone*
> *Billy Boy, Billy Boy?*

I sing softly. I could be the good baby. But I did not know how to be this charming Billy. I did not know how to be the good boy. I liked 'the man in the front row' my father called me. I liked the 'fast as you can, Ginger Man.'

First was boy and next was man but maybe next was soldier and maybe next the soldier did this killing kind of making dead. All this wrapped around my earliest fears and linked to my worry.

I sang away the worry:

> *Walking My Baby Back Home*

I sing loud, like the radio man. Like my daddy.

CHAPTER 4

The Secret

LENA HAD A SECRET to tell me. My secret places meant alone and I never told about them. But Lena's secret needed to be told and I was going to be the one that got told, but not until she came home from school on Friday. Before I would be even maybe told, I had to promise I would not tell this secret or even tell that there was a secret.

"Is it about your braces?" I asked. Lena did not like that she would be getting braces on her teeth. I did not know what that meant.

"No, silly Billy, it's not about my braces. You have to promise not to tell that I'm telling you and you have to promise not tell what the secret is."

"Yes," I said.

"Say yes, I promise."

"Yes, I promise," I said. It was my first secret and I wanted to be a good secreter. But it would not be told tomorrow because she had to go to the teeth dentist to ask about her braces. On Thursday Mrs. Norman was going to cut her hair so it would be told on Friday which was next and next.

School would be done again soon. My Bonnie Mom told Daddy Ray at dinner that my sisters had a very good year, or maybe they had been good for a year but they definitely had best grades and they definitely would pass, which was going to the next grade but not until after the summer. Next and after I thought, first it's next and then it's after. Maria and Carolyn and Joanne were on the honor roll at their school which was not sad but very good. Lena and Eleanor's school which was a grade school did not have a roll but it did have passing and they did pass.

There were lots of exciting next things before summer no school would be here. But the one that got the most talk, day after day was the junior prom. The junior prom had a dress, and a band which was music, and a boy. Joanne was asked, and you had to be asked or you couldn't go and you had to be asked by the boy. But then you needed permission which Mom was for and Daddy would be told about the permission at dinner and then he had to give it to Joanne.

Joanne was beautiful like Mom but she had Daddy's eyes and Daddy's hair but not really. She was taller than Mom already and she pulled her long hair back in a tail or unbanded it back and forth. She wore her picture smile all the time and she always noticed me first when I was around and tousled my hair and had a funny thing to say.

At dinner that night, Daddy's permission was easy. His mood had behaved and he teased and joked and rhymed. He pulled a small roll of paper from his pocket pretending it was the list of rules that the boy had to sign. These were promise rules and everyone laughed at each one and they went on and on and the paper curled in a pile on the floor so we could see that there was nothing on it. Joanne gave Daddy a big hug and even Bonnie Mom didn't rain.

But even with permission done there was lots more talk. Dress was a talk and then band was more talk. And then one evening at dinner Carolyn brought up a big talk. She had an ask too. She was only a freshman but she could go to the prom if she had an ask from a junior boy and guess what? She had one. But Daddy Ray said no. He said his no fast and maybe loud and Carolyn cried and left the table. Mom had a no too. A slower quieter no but still a no. Carolyn was too young which was just like being too little.

"Honey, even next year would be different. And you'll have your junior year and even your senior year," she said.

"This is Joanne's first prom," Daddy said. "It's not fair and you're too young."

"You treat me like a baby," Carolyn said. And this made her cry again.

"Well damn it, you're acting like a baby," Daddy said.

"Ray, that's not necessary," my mother said.

So Carolyn's permission was a no. When I was alone, I practiced Mom's word, necessary.

---

necessary

/ˈnesəˌserē/

adjective
required to be done, achieved, or present; needed; essential.

If there was a not necessary, then there had to be a necessary. I had to figure this one out. But it was clear that the baby that Carolyn was treated like was not the cutest little, was not a shoo shoo baby.

The days before the secret Friday were not good for Lena. She did not like what the teeth dentist told her about these braces and then the next day Mrs. Norman cut her hair and she came home crying. Mom cut my hair and I knew it didn't hurt so maybe Lena was just acting like a baby.

"Honey, it looks very pretty," Mom said, giving her a big hug.

"It's too short," Lena cried. "I look stupid." Stupid was a word no one was allowed to call anyone. It wasn't like a swear, but it was definitely bad.

"It doesn't," Carolyn said. "It looks cool. Everyone is going to be getting a haircut just like it."

"They'll call it the Lena," Maria said.

Eleanor found two bright blue barrettes that weren't a borrow but a present and Lena was happy after my sisters fussed around her, pinning them on each side.

Then it was Friday. After school, Lena found me outside by the pump.

"I have to change my school clothes, Billy," she said. "Meet me under the oak tree on the fence side and I'll tell you the secret."

This long waiting seemed to be a part of this secret thing and Lena planned the waiting to make her secret even better.

"Is it about your haircut?" I asked.

"No," she said. "Of course not."

"Is it about you going to the fourth grade? Because I already know that."

"Stop guessing, Billy or I won't even tell you."

I really wanted to be the one that was told so without another guess I headed down the hill and Lena ran into the house. When she met me where you could almost hide between the huge trunk of the oak tree and the fence, she had two of Mom's chocolate chip cookies, one for me and one for her. This secret thing was great and I was very excited.

"First you promise not to tell that you know anything."

"Yes, I promise," I said. Remembering that I couldn't just say yes and definitely couldn't say perhaps.

"Well, we're moving," Lena said.

"Who?" I asked.

"Us. All of us. We're moving to a new house where Daddy works because he bought it or he is going to buy it."

"He's going to buy a new house?"

"He's going to buy everything. The place where he works and the house and the fields, which is another property, and we're moving there."

"Well, what about our house?"

"We have to sell it."

Eleanor and Maria would sell boxes of cookies for the girl scouts, but I did not know that you could sell a whole house. I knew already that I did not like this secret, but I wanted to be nice. Also there were lots of parts that I did not understand. I told Lena this.

"I don't understand."

I had begun to ask more questions in these months after Daddy was home. And all of my sisters explained very slowly, especially about my stories during reading time. Except Lena. Lena did not like explaining and lately she just called me silly Billy and walked away. But not for this secret. Lena pulled out two more chocolate chip cookies and handed me one. I leaned my back against the big oak.

"Let me explain. You know Irwin Provision Company?"

"Where Daddy works."

"Yes. Well, he wanted to buy it and Mommy said it was better to work for yourself so then he did buy it with all of the buildings and a house to live in and two big fields."

"But why do we have to move?" I asked. I had only guessed at this word move, that it meant living in another place.

"Because Daddy has to sell our house to get the money to buy Irwin Provision Company and he said he would fix the new house and we could live in it."

"Is it broken?"

"It's not good, Billy." Now I realized that Lena did not like this move secret.

"It's old and smaller and I will have to go to a different school and so will Eleanor." Lena rubbed her face into her arm, trying not to cry and took another bite of her cookie. "Mommy said it's exciting and an adventure and that lots of people never get to work for themselves."

"I like adventures," I said. I was trying to make Lena feel better about her secret.

"Joanne and Carolyn don't care much because they still go to Hempfield High School but on a different bus and Maria still goes to Harrold Junior High."

"Your new school might be very nice," I said.

"Maybe. But I wanted to get Mrs. Dawson in the fifth grade because she's the nicest teacher in the whole school."

"Your new school might have the fourth grade teacher who's the nicest and that would be sooner." I still wanted to make Lena happy, but I was not happy about this secret either. I was confused and I did not like it.

"What about our things?" I asked.

"We take our things to our new house, silly."

This was the first time she called me silly, so maybe she was getting tired of explaining, but I had to ask when and I did.

"When?"

"Eleanor just said before school starts in the fall."

"Eleanor knows the secret?"

"She told me. Carolyn told Maria and Eleanor. Eleanor cried, mostly about leaving her school."

"Oh," I said, disappointed that this secret had already been told and told.

"Really, Billy, it will be fine." She stood up and kissed me on the top of my head.

"Really, Billy," I said. Lena laughed because she didn't know she had made a rhyme.

I watched her walk slowly up the hill and into the house. I headed for my secret place under the rose bush. I had to think about this move or moving. I had lots of questions and I needed my mind to do lots of explaining.

I climbed into my rose bush place and sat fixing a bridge that had broken since my last time here. Moving meant leaving in those first hours of thinking about Lena's secret. And even if we took our things to the new house, I knew that the things I loved the most I would have to leave behind: the pump and the grape arbor, the porch and the big grassy hill and especially my secret places and of my secret places especially the rose bush. But I liked adventures and Mom said it would be one. Besides, this moving was a long way away. The school-out summer vacation wasn't even here yet and before school starts was after a lot of afters. "Adventure," I said out loud. I'll find new secret places. I wouldn't cry like Eleanor. I wouldn't act like a baby.

Although everyone knew this moving secret, it was still never spoke about because of the promises. But I was the only good promiser, because I never told anyone.

One morning Mom went to Joanne and Carolyn's school because they were awarded and Mom wanted to see. But I was too little, so I had to stay with Mrs. Norman. She was very nice, even if she did cut Lena's hair too short. I didn't know why I was too little to just sit and see an awarded but Mrs. Norman gave me two cookies. She was very nice.

Then Mom went to Maria's school one evening after dinner because the house was open and Maria had a special drawing in the hall and she was going to sing with all her class, but I was still too little and Daddy had to stay home with me.

I have a real memory of that evening alone with my father. He is sitting at the piano. I am on the floor near his bench. He is playing, but it isn't a familiar song and he doesn't sing. I only knew then that it was a very, very old song. I know now that it was Beethoven's Moonlight Sonata. I am sitting so I can see my father's face and watch his large hands move over the keyboard. He stares directly ahead although there is no sheet music. He is playing the whole Piano Sonata #14 in C sharp minor. I sit silently, intently watching. At one point, I notice tears streaming down his cheeks but he does not stop playing nor try to wipe them away. It is when I wipe my own tears with my sleeve that I realize I am crying, motionless and silent, not like a baby. Not like a baby.

Finally there was a time when I could go to a school. It was Eleanor's school. She was in a play and I was going too. Eleanor announced this play at dinner and she was very excited and we all got excited for her because she had the lead which meant she gets to talk a lot. At first I did not understand this play thing. Eleanor and Daddy would play the piano and I would go out to play, but I did not know how you could be in a play. Joanne explained it to me.

"A play is like a story, but people pretend to be the characters on a stage."

"But how do they know what to say?"

"What they say is called their lines. And they're all written down for them and they memorize them. Then they say them on stage like people talking."

"Oh," I said.

"The characters wear costumes," Eleanor said. "I'm a princess and Mom's going to make me a princess costume with a crown and everything."

"Good," I said. "When do we go, tomorrow?"

"No," Eleanor said. "We have to rehearse every day at lunchtime and recess all month."

"We go next month," Mom said. "Just before school's out."

So seeing Eleanor's play became a next. But in my mind the big next was the secret move that everybody knew but kept silent and secret.

Joanne's prom finally came and she looked beautiful in a long shiny dress that Mom made, which was better than any store bought dress. Carolyn said she was happy for Joanne, which was nice since her ask didn't get a permission. Joanne was surprised at this prom, because she was queen, with a real crown, not like Eleanor's pretend crown.

I was very behaved at Eleanor's play but I could not understand it. I liked when the king's jester fell down with a big tray and the tin cups clattered to the floor and I liked seeing Eleanor say all her lines. But I knew I would rather be in a play than just be the one to sit and watch which was the audience. I clapped loudly when everyone lined up and bowed. I told Eleanor that I liked my first play and that I really liked her performance because Joanne told me to say that. But I did not know which thing was her performance.

When Daddy Ray finally announced the secret move he had another good mood. After dinner he told us all to come into the living room. He sat at the piano and played and sang *Sentimental Reasons*. After he finished my Mom moved, sitting on the corner of the piano bench and whispered, "I love you." And then Dad played *Zip-a-Dee-Doo-Dah*. And ended with a final stroke down all of the keys and began talking like a radio man.

"Now you all may be wondering why I asked you here this evening," he said.

Everyone laughed but I didn't know why. We lived here.

"Well I have a special secret announcement which I suspect has already been shouted from the highest hills."

Everyone laughed again, but I did not. I didn't want anyone to think I had shouted the secret or even told, which I didn't.

"We're going to move this coming August because the business property that we will soon own includes a house and we need to sell this house in order to buy the business."

"What's the house like, Daddy?" Maria asked.

"You'll all see it in due time, but it's small and it's not pretty like this house. But your Mom has made this house pretty, and I'll bet she'll make her magic on the new one."

"How small?"

"There's only two bedrooms upstairs," Mom said. "But they're large. The baby will sleep in with Lena and Eleanor and Joanne, Carolyn and Maria will share the other room."

"Where will you and Daddy sleep?" Carolyn said.

"We'll have to make the living room into our bedroom at night," Mom said. "But we'll use a pull out sofa and there will still be room for the piano and the radio. It's big really. The kitchen is huge too, although the sink is really old and the floor is a mess."

"And that's where the Bonnie magic comes in," Daddy said. "It's a good deal really. We'll be able to build on at the back, probably by next summer. There's lots of land, a garage, the shop. They're including the cattle truck, a pick-up truck and a delivery van. It's really a good deal."

"What's a good deal?" I asked.

"Well, Jack," my daddy said. "A good deal is when you got so little money that it isn't even funny but you still get a lot for the money that you've got."

"It's when you get lots of things for your money," Carolyn said.

"That's what I just said."

Then Daddy started playing *Zip-a-Dee-Doo-Dah* again, and we all joined in singing about all the sunshine and good feelings.

Afterward, Joanne told Carolyn that it was a bad sign when Mom and Dad used the word '*really*' that many times. When school was finally out and my fourth summer officially began, everyone was on board with the move. Maria said on board meant we were all for it, like on a train going on the same trip.

I was definitely and officially on board, ready for the adventure.

I was growing too big for my rose bush secret place but I still liked to go there. One day I stayed under the rose bush during a fast rain and I hardly got wet. But Mom said she was worried about me and why didn't I answer when she called.

"I didn't hear because of the rain and maybe I was singing," I said.

"Tell your mother you're sorry, Jack."

"I'm sorry, Mom," I said. And I was. I didn't want to be one of her worries.

Daddy drinking became one of Mom's worries that summer. She told Joanne she thought he drank too much and she worried about him. This was the kind of drinking that made you drunk and I guess she was worried he would fall down.

But still Bonnie Mom made some drinks for both of them one evening before they were going out dancing. Maria said they were all dolled-up and Daddy smelled very good.

"Have a seat," my mother told Daddy. "I'm going to make us the Stork Club's cocktail special. A little vodka, a little cream, some coffee liqueur and the secret ingredient."

Only she and Daddy could have these Great Alexanders because even Joanne and Carolyn were too little. I liked that they were too little too. Sometimes, by the pump, I would make the Stork Club special but it was only water.

One day, Daddy came home from work in a truck with an open back for hauling things, just like one I had, but big. In the back of the truck he had a big something covered with a huge cloth.

This is a real memory. I don't recall any stories about my father bringing home the new company sign before it was installed. My father

45

waited until everyone was home, just before dinner, then he had us gather outside by the truck. I'm standing in the front. I'm excited about what's under the cloth. My father is again using his announcer voice and he pulls off the cover with great flare. Everyone claps. Lena reads the sign to me: Calvin Provision Company. I had recognized Calvin, our last name. The letters are bright red outlined in dark blue. In one corner is that common graphic of a cow with the puzzle piece outlines designating the cuts of meat.

"It will go on the roof of the slaughter house," my father says. "And it will have two spotlights on it at night."

I remember moving back behind Carolyn. Everyone was voicing their admiration for the sign, but I was silent. After dinner sitting under the oak tree I said the word slaughterhouse out loud.

"Slaughterhouse." I didn't know what that meant, and I did not want to ask.

CHAPTER 5

Slaughterhouse

AS MOVING TIME neared, my fourth summer was coming to an end. I would turn four that coming January, but I began to think of my age as the number of cherished summers anticipated and remembered. Even as an old man looking ahead to my 78th summer I think of my age as 78.

We began putting stuff in boxes which was packing. I even had duties that Eleanor said were a big help. I liked when anything about me was big because I had heard people say I was small for my age but maybe because Daddy was so big.

Daddy was often home late, getting things ready at the business. Mom would keep his dinner warm in the oven. One time he didn't come home at all until the next morning and my Bonnie Mom was more than worried, she was mad.

"No Ray," she said. "This is not going to happen. Damn it. It is not going to happen."

"I'm sorry honey," he said. "I was going over the books in the office and I laid my head down on the desk, and then it was too late to call. I didn't want to wake everybody."

"Oh Ray you're still half drunk, so don't hand me these lame excuses."

"I went up to Beanos for a few beers, just a break."

"Ray, you don't even drink beer. I can't believe there's a damn bar at the top of the hill. But this is not going to happen, I won't put up with it."

"You're right. You're right. It won't happen." And then my daddy hugged away my mom's mad.

In the next weeks the maybe buyer people came to look at our house, walking through every room even my tiny room at the end of the hall which one lady said wasn't really a bedroom, but might make a good closet.

One family had a little girl my age and I helped by taking her out to the grape arbor and the pump. I even showed her how to make the pump work, and told her the bushes on the side of the house had big flowers in the spring and they smelled really nice. She had two brothers and two sisters and her mother liked that the house was really big. Her father liked the big porch and they both said that the oak tree and the rose bush were beautiful. I did not mention that they were my secret places because it was still a secret.

They bought our house and they said it was a good deal. I knew what that meant. Mom said it was a good deal for us too. We got more money than we had even hoped we'd get and it was time to move.

Lena was right. We did take all our things. They got loaded on to the big cattle truck that Daddy washed really good so it didn't even smell.

I hadn't seen the new house. Joanne or Carolyn stayed home with me while everyone else went to clean and get it ready. Maria said we really had our work cut out for us and I thought that was funny. When we left the old house for good, I rode on my mother's lap in the big truck. Joanne, who had gotten her driver's license drove the Buick and my sisters rode with her. I whispered goodbye as we backed out onto the road and Mom gave a little wave to the empty house, so I waved too.

I have odd and vague memories of first seeing the new house and business. There are black and white photos I have in an old album. They are labeled with a year and a word or two: Arona house 1947, cattle pen, shop, back-lot, smokehouse. I try to use these faded images to conjure a memory.

I recall my mother repeating the word solid to describe the house. Anytime one of them complained, my sisters would say to each other "But it's really solid," which made them laugh. These old photos of the house show a large cinder block building covered in stucco. Two concrete steps lead to a front door in the center. A staircase divides the house into four large rooms. So large, that all of our beds and dressers and stands from the five bedrooms in the old house easily fit into the two rooms we shared. The kitchen was below the bedroom I shared with Lena and Eleanor. The huge downstairs room opposite the kitchen could fit the piano, the old radio, the tall wardrobe, the sofa and chairs from our living room and the new sofa that changed into a bed.

I have a vague memory of feeling an emptiness for what I left behind, the rose bush, the grape arbor and my tiny sleeping room at the end of the hall. But the sharpest memory that returns to me hangs again on the same single word, baby.

All of the ways I had wrestled out of my baby title returned. I felt it in the caution of Bonnie Mom's new rules.

"The baby can't be by himself in the front. There's no fence and cars are coming in and out for the butcher shop," she said. "Hey Baby Doll," she would warn. "Watch those stairs. They're much steeper than the ones at the old house." "Joanne, check on the baby," she would call.

My old freedom was gone. This babying made a wall between my father's world of the butcher shop and my mother and sisters' world of the house.

Soon my sisters were back in school again. They had to walk down our road across the small creek bridge and up the steep hill that connected the dirt road to the paved one where the bus stopped. Lena liked her new school and her teacher. Eleanor did too. She liked being in the sixth grade and already talked about going to the Junior High School next year on the other bus. And Joanne was a senior and would graduate which means she'd be done.

routine

/roo̅ˈtēn/

noun

a sequence of actions regularly followed; a fixed program.

My new favorite word was routine. Bonnie Mom said we had to learn a new routine and Carolyn talked about getting used to the routine and Maria announced at dinner that she had settled into her routine. I didn't have a routine but I wanted one.

"Get with the routine, Jack," my father said one morning.

I was sitting on the staircase in my pajamas trying to fix a wheel on a small toy car.

"I don't have a routine," I said.

"That's just it, Jack," he said. "The Daisy Mae's are all off to school and you're still sitting there in your pj's."

"Pj's?" I said.

"Go get dressed. Fix your cereal. Then go out back and chop some wood."

"Chop wood?"

"Okay," he kissed the top of my head. "There's no wood to chop, but go play in the back field."

"Is that safe, Ray?" my mom said.

"Sure. It's all fenced in."

"Stay within the fence, Baby Doll."

"Yeah, Baby Doll Jack, stay inside the five acres. Really Bonnie."

I had my freedom back and I had a routine. That morning distance became a secret place. A shallow stream ran across one side of our back field and there I built my own country with towns and roads, bridges and dams, houses, stores and schools. My mother's call was a faint drawn out song of my name, "Bill-y." This meant to come back to the house because I couldn't answer loudly enough for her to hear.

Because my Bonnie Mom is also helping in different ways with the new business, I am alone more than ever in these months before I would start school. Starting school was my new next, my new sense of future, although it was nearly two years away, half a lifetime.

While I still loved the privacy in the places that distance gave me, I began to think of place as the named towns and states, mountains and rivers. We lived in Arona, in Pennsylvania, in the Allegheny Mountains, near the West Virginia border. I'd lie in the wild grasses of the far field and stare at the sky. I would imagine a view of myself from the clouds, and it was at this time that I learned of my favorite place word, *Earth*.

Earth
/ərTH/

noun
the planet on which we live; the world.

Earth was the biggest place name I knew then. I'd run as fast as I could to the furthest fence in the back field, down across a bank where a small orchard of plum trees backed into a steep mountain of slate. There were three other houses on our dirt road, but you couldn't see them from anywhere on our property. Here our house and the other buildings were also out of sight. I would sit and think, I'm on the Earth. I didn't know the word gravity, but I felt this pulling connection to the ground I sat on. I didn't know the Earth turned on its axis and circled the sun. But I felt that this earth was a greater aloneness than the hidden world under the rose bush, a wonderful private connection to the center of me. I could lie back and almost feel the spin of the planet as it passed the heat and light of the afternoon sun. At night I would lie on the ground in the front yard with Lena and Eleanor and sometimes Joanne. We would watch the blackness jeweled with these far away suns.

Soon, Bonnie Mom did work her magic, and the new house became our house and then just home. Everything got painted. The bedrooms were blue and the entrance and stairway was a bright white. But most amazing was her magic in the huge kitchen. The other owners had left what Daddy Ray called the Franklin stove, but you didn't cook on it. It was a big black iron box with a door on it. On those early fall mornings there would be a blazing fire in it like in the fireplace at our old house. It sat in the middle of the back wall. There was a window on each side, where I could see the sun rise over the far hills. Now the old Franklin looked shiny new against bright yellow walls. For each of the windows, Mom had made pale yellow curtains with blue pears. Of course I knew that pears weren't really blue. Our stove and our refrigerator and cabinets were all brought from the old house and Daddy Ray surprised Mom with a new sink that got hooked up where the old one was. And guess what? The floor man came and he remembered me. He rolled out a bright new floor with deep yellow blocks and black blocks and white circles around the edges. Our table kept all four leaves in it since the room was so big. And now it was right in the middle with four more chairs.

"That makes a dozen," Lena said. Explaining to me it meant twelve.

One Saturday morning everyone was up and in the kitchen. There was a fire in the old Franklin and Mom was cooking bacon and pancakes on the gas stove.

Daddy had already been outside and came in loudly singing 'Oh what a beautiful morning.' "I started starved and your mean mother is making me even hungrier with all these smells," he said. Moving around the room he kissed each of my sisters on the top of the head calling out, "Mornin' Daisy Mae."

"We're having flapjacks, Jack," he said to me. "Check out this sun rise." He lifts me up, although he usually said I was too big to be carried. He stands at the window with me in his arms. We stare out at the sun, just becoming visible over the far hills. The green trees had started turning yellow and red and orange. The smell of bacon and pancakes fills the room which is almost hot. He sings softly in my ear in his fine tenor voice:

In a canyon, in a cavern.
Excavating for a mine.
Lived a miner, 49er.
And his daughter, Clementine.

"Let's put the phonograph and the radio in the kitchen." Carolyn said. "There's plenty of room."

"Great idea," my daddy said. He put me down.

"They'll both fit near the hoosier," my mom said.

"I'll get the tables, Daddy," Joanne said.

In minutes the phonograph and radio were set up in the kitchen where they stayed as long as I can remember.

Joanne turned on the radio as soon as it was plugged in. Like magic, we heard the voice of Bill Adams say "Hello Pretenders." We all laughed. It was my favorite radio show, *Let's Pretend*. It wasn't a continued story like many of the programs. It was like the stories that were read to me, it had a beginning and a happy ending. We sat around the table, eating and listening to the story.

This is a memory made of many memories and it is part of my happy childhood, the part that is walled away from my fears, the part that is nurtured by the rising suns and the star-filled nights.

To me the Earth place was a secret. If someone asked me where I lived, I'd say Arona, Pennsylvania. The town had two coal mines, coke ovens, a grocery store and a post office. Our house and business down the dirt road wasn't in the town. It wasn't really a town. Not like where we moved from. That town had other houses and sidewalks and street lamps and different kinds of stores. Arona was just a dozen or so houses, the coal mines and the grocery store next to the post office where we got our mail. But we didn't even live in this town which wasn't really a town.

I loved the two mountains of slate, one which bordered the property to the back of our house, and the other even bigger one that started across the creek and after the railroad tracks. But they were off-limits. Off-limits was Bonnie Mom's word and I liked it too. It meant you couldn't go there or you couldn't do it.

"They're not real mountains," Lena said.

"You mean they're pretend mountains," I said.

"They're off-limits to you," my mother said.

"Aye aye sir," I said, saluting. I have a memory of using this Marine term which means, yes I understand the orders and I will carry them out. But I don't know where I would have heard it.

"Well they're not mountains at all," Eleanor said. "It's just where they dump the slate that's left over after they take all the coal out."

"Danny Pulski and his brothers take a bucket and pick out the coal that's still good," Lena said. "Can we do that?"

"No, we'll get another truck load of coal for the furnace when it gets colder," Mom said. "I don't want you girls on the slate dumps either."

Our driveway and the parking lot for the butcher shop were also off-limits. One day a dump truck brought loads of red-dog, coming back three times. A plow leveled it all before a steam roller packed it down smooth. I was allowed to watch all of this from our front yard which was sometimes off-limits. There was a joke about a steam roller that would make me laugh until I would start to hiccup.

Lady, Lady, your son just got run over by a steam roller.
I'm in the bath tub. Just slip him under the door.

I had never seen a cartoon, but this funny kind of making dead that didn't worry the lady both nudged a fear and eased it at the same time.

With my older sisters, I could explore some of my other off-limit places. Joanne would take me down to the cattle pen, a large fenced-in area that connected to the slaughter house by a series of narrow fences. There were also sheep and hogs but I liked the cows because they would come up to the sturdy wood rails and I could touch them. There were no calves which could be made into veal because Daddy Ray said he couldn't kill calves, though lots of people wanted to buy this veal. I tried not to think what he could kill but I still did sometimes think it and I didn't like it.

I liked the smells of the smokehouse which my mom let me see.

"Never touch these doors," she said. She unlatched the double metal doors. "They're cool now but they get very hot when it's smoking." She pointed out the sausages and slabs of bacon and hams hanging on heavy metal hooks. "These are our specialties," she explained. She said it was good to have a specialty, but I didn't have one.

The business had five workers that did stuff in the smokehouse and the butcher shop where customers came to buy the meat. One worker just delivered the meat to other stores and restaurants. Joanne said business was booming, but I never heard it.

Two different workers came and built a fence all around our front yard and painted it white. The weeds were all cut down and there was a gate built that you unlatched to get to the butcher shop, the parking lot, and the other buildings. Now the front yard was always on-limits but unlatching the gate was definitely not.

---

slaughterhouse
/ˈslôdərˌhous/

noun
a place where animals are slaughtered for food.

I'm an old man, trying to find the words of long ago before I lose the words I have now. There is a memory connected with the word slaughterhouse. Can I remember it? Can I invent it? Before I became inured to the daily activities surrounding Calvin Provision, before I began a routine of my own adolescent duties, there is a gnawing, vague memory.

"What's up, Jack?" my father says.

I'm sitting outside on the front steps. It's a comfortable day for early December, a few months after we moved here.

"Nothing's up," I said.

"Come on. I'll show you the ropes of the business. You'll be taking over in a couple of years."

"I have to go to school pretty soon."

"Well okay, but after third grade you can take over."

"Okay, I'd like to see the ropes."

"Now your mom's right. Don't be crossing through the parking lot by yourself. There are trucks backing out and customers pulling in."

"Aye, aye sir."

"So we start out at the cattle pen," Daddy explained.

I climbed up the fence rails so I could see good. There were four cows still in the pen. I watched Daddy Ray prod one of the cows into the narrow fencing that led into the slaughterhouse.

"Okay, go around to the front, I'll meet you."

The large bright red sliding door to the slaughter house was open. I had seen the concrete room with all the iron rails on the ceiling and the big refrigerator with the sides of beef that were ageing which didn't tell their age, just how tender the steaks were. But I had never seen a cow standing in the tiny tight fence. I had never seen a cow waiting. He was mooing, and mooing.

"To be safe, you wait outside while I shoot."

He slid the big red door closed, and I stood outside. The gun shot wasn't very loud, but I jumped when I heard it. My daddy pulled the door half open and I saw the cow lying on the concrete floor.

"Don't worry. He's dead," Daddy Ray said. He had already looped the rope around the cow's back legs, and the loud hum of the overhead machine began as the cow was raised into the air upside down.

"Here, you can work it." He handed me the pulley. "Just pull on this side for up." I did and the cow rose toward the ceiling.

"Okay, stand back," he said. "Here. You're in charge of the hose. Just make the water run in the trough drain."

Then Daddy Ray took a long knife and slit into the cow's throat. His hand was dripping with blood, and he rinsed it in the water running from my hose. His high boots and long rubber apron were splattered red and he stepped back while the hot steamy blood poured onto the concrete.

I stared into the water stream coming from my hose. A silent scream lodged deep inside me, a baby scream, primal and hot surrounded by the sweet smell of the killing blood. A scream buried deep inside my baby fears. Men kill. Boys become men. Men kill.

> *Where have you been Billy Boy, Billy Boy?*
> *Where have you been charming Billy?*

I heard my mom calling me.

"Go ahead; see what your mom wants."

"Okay."

"We got a little time to get you up to speed before you take over. I'll watch you cross the lot." He slid the big red door completely open. "Run, run," He called.

"As fast as you can," I answered.

"Where have you been, honey?" my mom asked.

"I was helping Daddy."

"So what did you do?"

"I held the hose."

"You hungry? I'm going to heat up some of that lentil soup."

"Okay."

That night at bed time I noticed a tiny spot of blood on my shoe. I rubbed it off with my sleeve.

CHAPTER 6

School

I HAVE NO MEMORY of that first Christmas in the new house or my fourth birthday that January, but I recall clearly with all the details of that exciting waking morning, the first snowfall. I woke up early. It was probably late December just before we changed the year to 1947. I went to the window in my room and then ran downstairs to the kitchen window. It's too early for the light of dawn, but the brightness of the full moon is reflected off the mounds of drifting snow. The air is clear and still. I watch the occasional wind blow flaky wisps from the trees. Now the slate dumps really are mountains. Snow covered peaks, rising from the real Allegheny Mountains. I'm calling everyone's name. Yelling as loud as I can, I wake everybody up.

"Goddamn, Jack, what's going on?"

"Honey, are you okay?" Mom gave me one of her hand paddles that doesn't hurt but means I've not behaved. "You scared me half to death."

"Half to death?" I said. "Look Mom, how beautiful." My sisters are downstairs now, crowding to the window, still pulling on robes and tying ties.

"Look, look." I tell each one.

The beauty, the amazing moon beauty of the snow silences us all for seconds. Enough seconds to hear the wind and see it push the flakes into a curving drift.

"What time is it?" Maria asked.

"Vacation time," Carolyn said.

"Too early to be up," Eleanor said.

"Flap Jacks time," Daddy said.

"Flap Jacks, Flap Jacks." Lena began a chant and Eleanor and I join in.

"Okay, I'll make pancakes," Mom said. "If, after breakfast, we all go back to bed. It's Sunday, sometimes called the day of rest."

"A deal. Flap Jacks and back to bed," Daddy said.

"I'm not getting back to sleep now," Joanne said. "I'll make a fire in the Franklin."

"Turn on the radio," Eleanor said.

I would check at the window to see the grey light slowly increase. The heavy wet snow clung to the sinking tree branches. After breakfast, Lena and Joanne and I went outside. The lower field could be a fast ride on a sled down the steep hill to the meadow, but that day the snow was too deep. We made a snow man in the front yard.

"Okay, I'm ready to go back to bed now," Joanne said.

"Me too," Lena said.

I sat on the floor in front of the Franklin stove alone. Then even I went back to bed.

Saturdays were the best. When Lena and Eleanor didn't have to go to school, they played school. Since they were the teachers, I got to be the student. I learned to count to one hundred. But my favorite learning was all the letters, called ABC's, and sometimes called the alphabet.

"Name a word that starts with an A," Eleanor said.

"Apple." I said.

"Good, now a B."

"Balloon."

"A word that starts with a C."

"City," I said.

"Wow," Lena said. "How did you know that?"

"From my poems."

In my mind, I told myself a something that day. I did my own explaining. It was the connection between the words, the wonderful, singing, rhyming, magical words and the letters that made them. Now I had a real routine. Every day I would go through my favorite poems from the *Junior Instructor*, poems I knew by heart, and check the words with the printed alphabet that Lena had made for me. Slowly, very, very slowly, I was able to make out new words.

To discover reading, alone, as an unraveled mystery, is a kind of wonder that I've never repeated in all my decades. This is a collapsed memory of a daily routine that went on for months. With Lena and Eleanor I had learned the sound that each letter stood for and combinations of sounds that Lena called buddy letters. The S and the H and the T and the R could be buddies and make a new sound together.

When I could pronounce the words, the letters became invisible, then the words disappeared into another whole that sent me a rhyme, and I laughed. There is one separate memory in those months of teaching myself. I'm sitting on the floor of the new living room, so it had to be after my fifth summer, when they completed the two story addition. There is a fire in the fireplace so it was late fall or early winter. I'm working on my reading which is almost a daily routine. The ways in which letters combine into words now has an ease to it. It is a poem, but the lines do not rhyme. I feel first the rhythm of the words connecting into this unsung kind of song. And then I feel inside me a kind of message. Perhaps it is a short Edna St. Vincent Millay or a Robert Frost poem. I don't know. It's an odd sad thing it's telling me. I repeat the words again out loud. It's a reminder that all the pushed down confusions can be in me and I still can be safe, warmed by the burning logs in our fireplace, warmed by the wordless music coming from the kitchen, warmed by these letters, these words, these sentences, these messages. I can read.

One day I heard my mom talking to Joanne.

"Your father's drinking again." I had forgotten about Mom's Stork Club special drinks that she never made anymore. With the new business,

Daddy Ray didn't have time to play the piano and sing for drinks. I hadn't thought that Daddy didn't drink now.

"Oh darn," Joanne said. "He was doing so great too. When?"

"I thought he might have been drinking on Tuesday. He smelled like mouthwash before dinner."

"Darn," Joanne said again, which wasn't a bad word.

"He didn't come home last night."

"What are you going to do?" Joanne asked.

"I'll have to get Bart to take over in the slaughterhouse. I'll help out in the shop."

"No, I mean, what are you going to do about Daddy drinking?"

"Really, Joanne, what can I do? At least he can't get fired." I didn't know what fired was but it seemed like a good thing that Daddy couldn't get it.

When Daddy did get home, he was definitely what Mom called drunk. It was like this not drinking meant he had to drink a lot. And the drinking had to keep on going, and it did. Mom hid the keys to the car and the trucks but Daddy walked to the bar at the top of our hill.

Daddy Ray was quiet, almost silent during these drinking days. But Mom was loud. She was loud about her worry and really loud when he got sick in the kitchen. It was more than a week later before Daddy was not drinking, and he began working each day in the slaughterhouse.

Slowly his silence gave way with a whistled tune or a "What's up, Daisy Mae." Slowly Daddy Ray would find a funny joke or sit at the piano and play a wordless song. One evening he played the piano and sang. I came in the living room and sat on the floor by the piano bench.

"What's jumpin', Jack?" he said between singing.

"Nothin'," I said.

When Joanne went away to college, I cried. She said I could visit her at Grove City. I guessed that Grove City would be a whole city of trees.

"And *you'll* be going to school in the fall," Joanne said.

"Perhaps," I said.

"I thought you wanted to go to school."

"No. I can read now and Maria helped me make my letters."

"So you're thinking you can just skip this whole school thing."

"I guess not," I said.

The when of all this is very confusing. I'll be 78 and I feel a panic about the daily things I can't remember, and a widening veil of depression that keeps drawing me back to sorting out these early years. I know that Joanne had been awarded a scholarship when she graduated and she had a choice of schools. She took classes at a college she could drive to for a year or maybe just half of a year. I do know that I was starting school that fall when she left.

"You're going to love school," Joanne said.

"I don't think so."

"You play it all the time with Lena and Eleanor."

"I can't tie my shoes," I said.

"Hey, silly Billy, there's no shoe tying in school."

"Okay," I said.

"You're going to be great." She kissed me. After Daddy put more suitcases and boxes in the back seat and she climbed in the front with him, I cried again. I cried while I watched the car disappear up our road. My mom cried too. She bent down and hugged me.

"Ask Carolyn to show you again how to tie your shoes. She's a really good shoe-tier," Mom said.

I do remember that the idea of going to school changed from the thing I wanted most, to a thing I did not want at all. Most shoes had laces then. Although Carolyn and Maria and even Lena had shown me again and again, I couldn't get it. I worried that my shoe would come untied and like my mom warned me, I would trip. But more than that, the other kids would know I couldn't do this tying thing. I worried in general about other kids. And Daddy did too.

"He spends too much time alone, Bonnie. He really should be with other kids," Daddy Ray said.

"Well there's no other kids his age around," Mom said. "There weren't really any in Newburgh either."

"I guess only crazies like us made babies in the middle of a war."

"Accidental Babies," Bonnie Mom said.

"Dave Robbins has a boy about Billy's age. I'll ask him to bring him over some Saturday."

I wondered about Mom and Daddy making babies that were me. I knew accidents weren't good and I wondered about that too. But mostly I wondered about this other kids thing. And then one Saturday during the summer before I went to school, Dave Robbins did bring his son Jeff to spend the day.

Jeff had already turned six and I wouldn't be six until January. We both would start school that fall, but different schools. He brought a ball and bat and his leather glove and one for me that was too big for my hand.

The lower field had been mowed by a tractor, and Jeff loved that the wide meadow could almost fit a whole baseball diamond and would make a great football field. I had never played baseball, although I had rubber balls that I bounced off the side of the garage and a soccer ball that I sometimes kicked around. I couldn't throw good enough for Jeff to bat the ball and I couldn't catch it when he threw it to me.

"Play far back and I'll bat you some flys," Jeff said. I moved far down the field. "No, further back," Jeff called. I moved really far back and Jeff did get the ball to me, but I couldn't catch it and I had to run back toward him before my throw could reach. This wasn't fun for Jeff because it took so long, and it wasn't fun for me.

Jeff was taller than me and weighed a lot. He couldn't run fast so I bet I could beat him in a race and I did. I climbed trees higher than he could and called for him to get up to me. Just before dinner I showed him how to stand on the fence and lift yourself onto the flat garage roof.

"Come on," I called from the roof. "Just push up and swing your leg."

"I don't think I can," Jeff said.

"Come on. It's a great view. I do it all the time."

Jeff didn't make his last try and he scraped his knee tearing his pants and making it bleed. He started to cry which really surprised me. We had to go in and tell Mom. At least he had stopped crying but I still got yelled at because the garage roof was off limits. Jeff stayed for dinner and my sisters asked him lots of silly questions, but he answered them politely.

Jeff's visit made me more worried about the other-kids part of school and before I even knew anything about what school would be like, I definitely didn't want to go.

The only part of that first day of school that I recall is the bus ride. I know I started out early with Lena because our bus came a few minutes before the other one and Lena said I walked slow. Maria would later talk about how small I looked trudging up the steep hill to the road. The bus was my first experience with a whole group of other kids but none of them were starting the first grade. Lena wouldn't sit with me and she didn't want to talk with me. Her friend Kathy had saved her a seat, and I had to squeeze in beside a girl who didn't want me to sit there. We were the last stop before school but the ride seemed to never end.

School memories have no stories from family and at that time only the one class photo. The daily repetition meshes the recollections together and there is an odd insignificance to the things that can be recalled years later. I know that nothing calmed my fears or changed the dread of going to school that year.

Recess was softball and other kinds of ballgames. There were enough boys that soon I wasn't allowed to play. I felt I had to argue about this although I didn't want to play anyhow. The girls didn't want me to play with them, so I'd hang around the sidelines and pretend to cheer a good catch or a homerun.

I sensed early on that I shouldn't let the teacher know that I could read. And this caution was a worry. I think the teacher's name was Miss Parson or Carson, she was young but not nice like my sisters.

She was strict about going to the bathroom which was an outdoor toilet above the playground. One day she yanked a boy from his seat who had peed his pants. She made him wipe the seat with rags from the hall closet and stand out in the hall until the bus came which wasn't that long. He didn't cry which I thought was good but the whole thing made a little girl cry and she had to stand in the corner.

I remember I couldn't spell and that became my biggest worry. I would claim I was sick on the day of spelling tests but that very quickly didn't work. If I was slow getting ready, Lena would leave without me and sometimes I would miss the bus. I think this happened often, more than a few times anyhow. But then Mom made Daddy get up and drive me to school. This wasn't good either, because he didn't like that and we rode there in a gruff silence.

One time the teacher was passing back the spelling tests and she held mine up for all the kids to see the failing grade.

"So this is why you didn't want to come to school. Why you missed the bus."

I sat there silent. Yes that's why, I said in my mind. That's definitely why.

As reading lessons advance, I could reveal more and more that I was a good reader and parts of school became nice. I could memorize and knew answers if called upon but I never raised my hand. I tried to behave but I would forget and go to sharpen my pencil without permission or call Miss Parsons 'Mrs.' which she didn't like.

In general the memory of that school year is a flat and singular worry, even though I learned to tie my shoes before it ever became a problem.

Home was harder too that year. Lena didn't want me around and she sometimes yelled at me. When Daddy was drinking, Bonnie Mom worked in the butcher shop more. She waited on customers and did the books, though I didn't know what that was. She had ideas about the shop and it got painted white with a red ceiling. I helped paint the office door red. She had weekly specials and in the newspaper there was an ad with our name. It read, *Calvin Provision Company. Custom meats cut to your satisfaction.* I liked the word satisfaction but I didn't know when to use it.

satisfaction
/ˌsadəsˈfakSH(ə)n/

noun
fulfillment of one's wishes, expectations, or needs, or the
pleasure derived from this.

It seemed that Bonnie Mom didn't mind Daddy drinking so much and having to take over the shop. That drinking lasted weeks instead of days and then he wasn't drinking, and he was very sorry and very good. But it took much longer for him to return to rhyming, joking Daddy Ray and he hardly ever sang anymore.

I wake up and my dreams disappear and I can't even remember them. But this one stayed in my mind or maybe I dreamed it again and again until it stayed. That first time I am sleeping on the sofa in the living room. I wake up crying, screaming a cry. I had peed my pants which I never did and wet the sofa. I am comforted; not yelled at.

"I think he's sick," Carolyn said. My temperature is taken.

"It's normal," Mom said.

"He had a nightmare," Maria said.

I knew that word nightmare, a bad dream. "I'm okay," I said. I don't say anything about this dream. In the dream I'm lying on my stomach in a dirt bank. There are guns and explosions going off around me. I'm digging into the dirt with my little blue shovel. I've gotten my body into a shallow hole when a man comes at me. I pull out a knife and stab at him. I wake when I see the blood covering my hand.

One day when my claim of being sick didn't work, I yelled at my mom as she hurried me and Lena out the door. "I hate school," I said. "I hate school."

CHAPTER 7

Good

deportment

/dəˈpôrtmənt/

noun

a person's behavior or manners.

SCHOOL WAS BAD. I was bad. I didn't know you could be bad by not being able to spell or hit a ball, by sharpening your pencil or knowing the answer without raising your hand. I wanted to be good and I didn't want to be one of Mom's worries. But I was bad, and she did worry.

"Billy's not doing well in school," she told Maria.

"He's so smart. He reads everything."

"I know. He's always asking what some word means. Some of them I don't even know."

"He doesn't seem happy," Maria said. "That's for sure."

"You girls all loved school."

"I guess school's easier for girls. Have you talked with his teacher?"

"She said he doesn't pay attention."

Pay attention. Yes that's what Miss Parsons said to me too; pay it, like you paid money. I knew it meant listen, but I *did* listen. Some kids read aloud very slowly. Miss Parsons would tell them a word they couldn't sound out, but she told it like she was mad at the word. I'd read ahead or study the pictures. When she called my name, I wouldn't know where the class was in the story.

"Pay attention," she would say in a loud voice. Sometimes she would walk up the aisle to my desk. She'd turn the page back and point to the paragraph. I wanted to be good. But there were so many ways to be in trouble with Mrs. Parsons, I mean Miss Parsons. See, that would be one. Mrs. was wrong. Anything could go wrong. My letters didn't come out inside the lines, too high, too low.

"This will have to be done again. This is not satisfactory."

She gave us letter grades on our report cards and I got F's in spelling and penmanship and a D in arithmetic. I got a C in reading even though I read aloud the best of anyone. It was because I didn't pay attention. On the card there was a part that said deportment. A whole list of things said all of the ways I hadn't behaved.

It didn't help that my sisters all got A's and had excellent deportment with nice notes at the bottom. My note said I had to focus. The whole school year was like that, and Mom was worried. But she was extra nice to me about it, and so were my sisters. My dad said he would teach me how to make the sausage. It was a joke, but I didn't laugh. Eleanor tried to help me.

"Focus is like listening and thinking carefully," she said.

"I do."

"Like last week, when I was helping you with your adding."

"I remember."

"In the middle of it, you asked me how the Earth knew to tilt back toward the sun when the winter was here and it was time to go to spring."

"You said you didn't know."

"That's not my point, Billy. You weren't focused on the adding."

"I just wondered how," I said.

"You need to pay attention to what you're doing," Eleanor said.

"I just wondered how."

relieved
/rəˈlēvd/

adjective
no longer feeling distressed or anxious; reassured.

When the school year finally ended, I was passed to the second grade and my mom was relieved. Relieved was one of my favorite words for a long time. It was like not holding your breath, like someone finally smiling, like the rain stopping when you wanted to go outside. By the time the Earth had tilted closest to the sun, and knew somehow to start back again, school had been out for weeks and relieved was freedom, my old glee from deep inside me. It was a good summer, but then it was bad, and then it was very bad.

Of course all of my sisters had passed too and now Lena would ride on the second bus to the junior high school. Carolyn was going to be a nurse but she still lived at home. Joanne was staying at Grove City because she had a job and she could take two courses which were lessons about one thing.

I could go to the store by myself that summer and to the post office just up from the store. That meant that all the places between our house and the store were no longer off limits, except the slate dumps and the road into the lower mine.

———

tipple
/ˈtipəl/

noun
a structure where coal is cleaned and loaded in railroad cars or trucks.

Tipple Road was the best way to get to the store. It wasn't used for trucks anymore, and you couldn't drive on it because on one side it stopped being a road and was just a path. It climbed like a steep ramp from our road, just across the creek, to a flat stretch that went for more than a mile. Lena said it wasn't nearly a mile, but it went a long way. On one side the steep bank led down to the creek. On the other side was another steep drop to the railroad tracks, where the train cars used to stop and get the coal. The tipple was at the far end of the road, its wooden parts half rotted, the machinery rusted and stilled. It wore the sag of defunct like the faded sign at the lower mine: Danger defunct mine. No trespassing.

Tipple was not a good word. It just meant that thing at the end of Tipple Road that once shifted the coal and loaded the train cars. But defunct was a great word. Defunct could mean extinct, like the dinosaurs. Ours was a dinosaur town.

The old man sits by the fire, always the fire; the heavy dictionary is propped on his lap, the lamp pulled from the corner to spotlight the pages. He reads aloud, "Defunct describes something that used to exist, but is now gone." A useful word he thought.

When I got to the flat part after the climb, I would run the whole mile to the end of Tipple Road breaking the finishing line string with my chest, sitting breathless as the crowds cheered. Coming home from the store, I sometimes would balance on the rail of the tracks, which wasn't permitted, but the almost never passing trains could be heard a long way off and you could climb the bank to Tipple Road long before it actually passed.

"Billy, how did you squash the bread like this?" my mom said.

I couldn't say that I had held it under my arm so I could balance perfectly on the rail and never fall off once from start to finish. "I don't know," I said.

"Did you get the mail?"

"I forgot."

"Billy."

"I can go back. I can."

"Okay, after lunch. But please, try not to squeeze the bread like this." And Mom grabbed me and squeezed me in a big hug, which made me sorry that I lied about not knowing how the bread got squashed.

Going to the post office was an errand. You ran errands, and I ran them as fast as I could. Not like the gingerbread man, that was too baby.

When Tipple Road turned into a path, there was a place where you could cross through next to the baseball diamond at the playground. It was a shortcut to the store and post office and I always took it. I never played ball. They said I was too little even though Jimmy Polski's brother played and he was just going to start first grade next fall. I got to play once when the teams were uneven but then another kid came and they said I couldn't. I was an easy out and I couldn't catch the ball in the way back field though it almost never came to me. Another day they promised I could play if I got on first in an up to bat test, and I did, but then they said I couldn't. I said a promise is a promise but I didn't cry. One kid said I was a cry baby. But I didn't cry. I just said a promise is a promise a few times. I didn't really want to play anyhow.

There were lots of places to explore in our dinosaur town. In places the creek was shallow enough to be crossed on stones and fallen logs. On that side of the creek was a whole town of old foundations where houses must have been homes to quadruple the people who lived here now. That's four times as many but maybe it was even ten times as many. Our box number at the post office was the highest, 27. Just twenty seven families left. Defunct was a good word. One place in the creek was deep enough to swim. It was between the walls of a bridge that wasn't there anymore and there wasn't a road either and you couldn't figure out where the road might have come from or where it might have gone to. It was all defunct.

The coke ovens that lined the hill on the other side of our road were crumbling ancient monuments that were built by the Aztecs or the Incas maybe. Inside the igloo-like stone ovens with their perfectly rounded domes, I built sacrifice mounds with sticks and sheets of slate.

The old man sits by the fire. He reads about these artifacts of the 19th century. "The iron and steel industries were made possible by these hills of black gold." He remembers the beautifully crafted coke ovens, each stone placed perfectly to create these miniature cathedrals, crumbling back into the nature that preceded them, catching his boyhood imagination that placed them in another century, in another continent.

I was taller for sure that summer, but I never got measured. Daddy Ray would take me with him to the cattle auction across the border in West Virginia. I could explore by myself while he bought the cows and hogs and sometimes sheep. Even when I sat with him and watched real close, I couldn't see him make the bid that the auctioneer called out real fast. "Okay we got a truck full. Let's pull around and get loaded up," he'd say.

I didn't like the way they pulled and prodded the cows to get them into the fenced ring at the bottom of the bleacher seats. So I would explore around. It was a world of men completely different from the world of my mother and sisters or school with just the other kids and Miss Parsons. Daddy would give me money for the lunch counter, which was at the top of the bleachers. Mike, who took your order and cooked and made the coffee, would give me the telephone book's yellow pages from under the counter so I could sit high enough on the stool to reach. The bacon frying on the griddle pushed out the smells of dung and hay that were everywhere else in the auction ring.

"What'll it be, Mr. Calvin?" Mike said. Just like I was a grown up customer.

"I'll have the blueberry pie and coffee," I said.

"Good choice, I just baked that pie this morning." That was a joke 'cause Mike didn't bake the A&P pies. The coffee was mostly milk and I'd stir in two packets of the sugar. The stools turned so I could watch Daddy Ray in the bleachers.

"Watch close now," Mike said pointing to my father.

"I don't see anything."

"There. How he raised his finger up like that. And there, again."

"I see."

"And again and again. And sold. Your daddy just bought himself a fine angus," Mike said.

I laughed. "I saw it, I saw it," I said.

That was part of the good summer, but then there was the bad.

CHAPTER 8

Bad

DADDY SAID he was just taking the Buick to deliver a box of steaks to Palmer's, a restaurant in Norwin which was the closest big town with shops and restaurants and even a movie theater.

"Do you want to go?"

"Sure," I said.

"Go tell your mother."

We didn't talk much. Not even on the long trips to the auction. He'd ask me if I was thirsty or did I have to use the bathroom. Sometimes he'd point out something like a line of huge crows on a wire or a pony in the field. I answered questions in single words. My love of words didn't include talking. Although Daddy joked and teased, he didn't really talk either. Talking seemed to be a girl thing.

"Should I wait in the car?" I said.

"No, you can come in."

We had parked in the alley behind the restaurant and the door led into a huge kitchen. Three men were already chopping stuff and getting ready. The owner shook Daddy's hand. Everything he said was like an announcement.

"We get a big crowd booked for these Saturday brunches. This must be your boy."

"Billy, this is Al."

"Good morning, sir," I said. He extended his hand and I had to reach up to shake it.

"Listen, Ray, you saved my ass on this one. Jenkins really screwed me. He knows steak and eggs is the Saturday brunch seller. Last minute he calls and said he didn't get his delivery."

"We do all our own butchering."

"Well, these look great. If they work out you've got a standing order. Listen, you've got to try my Bloody Mary. I just mixed up a batch."

"It's a little early."

We followed Al through swinging doors into the restaurant.

"Brunch starts in fifteen minutes. This is the best Bloody Mary you've ever tasted."

The tables had white cloths and napkins and bunches of flowers in little bowls. A lady was putting forks and knives on each table and she asked me how was I doing. We sat at a long bar at one end of the room. Al gave me a Virgin Mary. It wasn't a nice thing to name a drink after Jesus' mother but the Bloody Mary name for Daddy's drink sounded terrible. Mom's Stork Club special, Great Alexander, was a good name. Daddy Ray drank two of Al's special drinks, but I couldn't finish mine.

"That was great, but we better get rolling here," Daddy said.

"Thanks again, Ray. I won't forget this."

---

stranger
/ˈstrānjər/

noun

a person whom one does not know or with whom one is not familiar.

We went out the front door to Main Street. The summer sun was almost overhead.

"I want to stop and see Patsy," Daddy said. I didn't know who Patsy was or where we would go to see him but we walked up to the next block and into a place called Norwin Tavern. The room was small and empty. The bar was the whole back wall with just booths on the other side except for a brightly colored juke box. Dad didn't introduce me to Patsy.

"Vodka on ice and a ginger ale here, a bag of chips and a buck in dimes." He handed me the dimes first. "See if you can make that juke box sing," he said. Two guys came in and they called the bartender Ron so I guess we were waiting for Patsy to get there. I put the dimes in my jeans' pocket and took my ginger ale and chips to a booth by the juke box.

I knew some of the songs. I played *Riders in the Sky* and Burl Ives singing *Lavender Blue* and *Baby It's Cold Outside* which was funny 'cause the day was hot again and people were saying it was going to be a hot summer. I still had a bunch of dimes left but I sat in the booth and opened my bag of chips. I watched Daddy Ray's back and though the bar was filling up he didn't talk with anyone so I guess none of them were Patsy. It was then that I thought, Daddy's drinking. I heard it in my head in Mom's voice, Daddy's drinking. I went back to the juke box to find two more good songs.

---

drunk
/drəNGk/

adjective
affected by alcohol to the extent of losing control of one's faculties or behavior.

When I told Daddy I was hungry he got me a bag of pretzels and gave me more dimes even though I still had a bunch in my pocket. I put more dimes in and told a woman who came over to the juke box to pick any songs she wanted. Now Daddy Ray was talking and his talking sounded drunk, like I had heard him at home. I had never seen him go from not drinking to drinking, from not drunk to drunk. I didn't even know what drunk was. But as I watched him, he seemed stranger or maybe he seemed to become a stranger, to be someone I didn't know. I felt shy and timid approaching him.

"Daddy, I'm tired," I said.

"You know where the car is, just behind Palmer's. Why don't you take a nap in the back seat. Cut back to the alley by the restaurant. Take a little nap."

"Okay," I said.

"And Billy." He almost never called me Billy.

"What?" I said.

"Lock the doors, okay."

"Okay."

The Buick was hot, but I climbed into the back seat. I locked the doors and stretched out. I lay there wet with sweat and I couldn't fall asleep. But then I did, a deep sleep with different dreams that switched and switched.

I woke up fast because of loud knocking on the car window. The dreams disappeared and I couldn't figure out where I was. It was a policeman knocking on the window. I had never seen a real policeman. But in my school reader there was a story with pictures about one who helped Sally and Jane get their kitten out of a tree.

"Unlock the door, son."

When I opened the door, I climbed out of the car. He was tall and serious.

"What's your name, son?"

"Billy Calvin." I didn't know why the policeman called me son. I wasn't his son.

"Where's your father, Billy?"

"He's waiting for Patsy."

"Did he lock you in the car?"

"No."

"How long were you in the car?"

"I was sleeping."

"How long?"

"I don't know."

"Where's your father waiting, son?"

"Up the block. Just through the alley and up the block."

"Show me." The policeman took my hand. When we started up Main Street, Daddy Ray was walking toward us. This was a bad thing. He walked funny and when he spotted us he tried to not walk funny and that was not good because it seemed normal and then it was a stumble. "Daddy," I called out before we got to him.

He tried to joke. "Hey sleepy Jack. You ready to go?" he said, as though I wasn't holding the hand of a policeman.

"The policeman woke me up," I said.

"Thank you officer."

"Mr. Calvin, did you leave your son locked in the car behind Palmer's Restaurant?"

"No, he was with me. Doing a couple of deliveries. He was tired and went back to the car. I told him to lock the car. I told him to." Daddy's talk was drinking funny. The policeman didn't let go of my hand.

"You're in no shape to drive, sir."

There was more talk and we had to go in the police car because of Daddy's shape which wasn't good for driving. We sat in the back and Daddy Ray put his arm around me and whispered something about how neat it was, but I was scared. I loved him for knowing I was scared and trying to cheer me up.

Mom showed up at the police station and I started to cry when I saw her. I don't know why. Maybe because I thought I had said the wrong things to the policeman and maybe because she had her hair pushed back behind her ears in that worry way. Daddy was in some kind of trouble and probably it was my fault. If I hadn't been tired and I hadn't slept in the Buick. I tried to wave when we left without him, but he didn't see me. Mike drove us back home in the delivery van. When I reached into my pocket and touched the dimes, I felt the crying start in me again but I held it back.

CHAPTER 9

Father

father

/ˈfäTHər/

noun

a man in relation to his natural child or children.

I STARTED TO THINK of Daddy Ray as Father during this time, because of Dick and Jane and Sally. "Hello, Father," said Dick on the telephone. "There is Father in a boat," said Sally.

The day we left Daddy Ray in the police station, I changed him into Father. Like Dick and Jane and Sally's father, he needed to be in charge. I still mostly called him Daddy, and still mostly thought of him as Daddy Ray. But I seldom called him. I only answered.

My mom changed her name for him from Ray to Dad to Father back and forth. "Ray, could you check that latch on the gate?" Or, "Tell your Dad dinner will be ready in half an hour." Or, "Your Father's not home yet." (which meant that there was a reason to worry). Or, "Your Father's drinking," (the worry settled). If one of my sisters told me, they would say, "Daddy's drinking," even though they usually called him Dad.

now

/nou/

adverb

at the present time or moment.

It strikes me as odd that this singular narrative that surrounded my relationship with my father was predicated on the notion of drunkenness. His cycle of sobriety and drinking binges, on the wagon, off the wagon, defined this new sense of him. Rhyming, singing, Daddy Ray receded in my mind, leaving remnants of the deepest love, buried with my confusion, mingling with my fears.

---

arrest

/əˈrest/

verb

seize someone by legal authority and take into custody.

There is a feeling in my belly that stayed for weeks after the policeman found me sleeping in the back seat of the Buick. It connected to the policeman and my father, something about the way they talked to each other. It seemed to me that Mom was always there. I mean she had a continued always without a beginning and that seemed to cancel the possibility of an ending. The parts of her, her lips or how her hands moved when she talked or her eyes squinted when she smiled were signals to me of a 'momness', that kept her steady and that steadiness kept me safe. But Daddy Ray entered into my life like an actor in Eleanor's play. And right from the start, he could change in the way pretend changed. And there was something, something that was like a thought, but not a thought that connected to the change time when I watched him go from not drunk to drunk that day waiting for Patsy. The change gave him the lines he had to say to the policeman and it connected to the warmth of the policeman's hand as he held mine, not letting go. Like he and not Daddy Ray would keep me safe. And this something sunk into my belly and I couldn't make it go away.

I wanted to be by myself, but Mom and Carolyn and Maria kept being with me. Maria even went with me to the abandoned coke ovens and we sat in my favorite one. It had a neat hole in the ceiling that made the sunlight narrow into a beam. We sat on the floor at the far end and watched the light beam come and go.

"Why did the policeman take me and Daddy to the police station?"

"I think there are laws about leaving children locked in a car," Maria said. "I don't think the policeman would have arrested Daddy if he hadn't been so drunk."

"He arrested him?"

"Yes, didn't you know that?"

"What's arrested exactly?"

"Well, it's when you break the law. You're charged with, well, breaking the law and you have to pay a fine and maybe you can go to jail."

"Will Father go to jail, Maria? Tell me the truth."

"Billy, I always tell you the truth. No it's done with. Dad had to pay a fine for public intoxication, and he joined AA to help him stop drinking."

---

intoxication
/inˌtäksəˈkāSH(ə)n/

noun

the state of being intoxicated, especially by alcohol.

It kept being like that. Instead of knowing things, there was just more questions about the things you didn't know.

"It was my fault for sleeping in the Buick."

"Don't be silly, Billy."

"That's what Lena calls me, silly Billy." Maria hugged me.

"No, you're not silly. The idea that it's your fault is silly. Look, the spotlight is back."

We sat in silence and watched the beam of light until a cloud turned it off.

"What's AA?"

"I can't remember what the A's stand for but it's meetings that Dad will go to and they'll help him to not drink."

"How can you need help to not do something?"

"I don't know, Billy. I really don't."

---

infinite
/'infənət/

adjective
limitless or endless in space, extent, or size; impossible to measure or calculate.

It was during that time that I realized that everything was bigger than I thought. Not bigger like infinite, a word that I loved. The Earth, the sun, the Milky Way and more galaxies after that and more suns because infinite means never ending. This bigger scared me. How could you know all the rules? Not just like Mom's rules or school rules, but laws and being in trouble in big ways. And then I was. It all started with Cappy McLaughlin.

CHAPTER 10

Very Bad

I LIKED CAPPY. He was younger than me, but just as tall. He was starting school in the fall and had a lot of questions about what it was like that I could explain.

I'd see him at the playground, though we'd never make plans to meet or anything. We'd swing at the same time or seesaw, but more times just sit on the benches talking.

Cappy was funny. He liked to swear as much as possible and he'd say funny things like "There was a bee in the outhouse and my old man got stung in the ass." His old man was his dad. He lived in one of the row houses but his was painted and fixed better than the others except for the steps that always had a board missing.

---

oath

/ōTH/

noun

a solemn promise, often invoking a divine witness, regarding one's future action or behavior.

One time we sat on the porch and Cappy's Mom gave us both a glass of water.

"This water tastes funny," I said.

"Hell, it ain't that bad. But it's not too cold, so someone must have just filled the goddamned pitcher. But hell, everyone's got rotten egg water. If it gets cold in the pitcher it don't taste so bad."

"We don't."

"Bullshit. Everyone's got it."

"We don't."

"Then what the hell does your damn water taste like?"

"Like nothin'. It tastes like water. It tastes good."

"You're a lyin' sonofabitch, Billy Calvin. The devil's marking down your lies and your ass is going to hell."

"I never lie," I said. And I didn't, except for tiny fibs. Truth was my number one word for awhile. Like on the radio: Truth, Justice and the American Way.

"I swear it's the truth," I said.

"Sonofabitch, Billy. You never swear."

"That kind of swear is like an oath."

"What the hell's an oath?"

"It's like a promise, but bigger. You raise your right hand. And maybe you put your other hand on a bible."

"Yeah, yeah," Cappy said. "I still doubt your water don't taste like nothin'. The whole town's got rotten egg water. How could you have some special water?"

When I asked Bonnie Mom about it, she said our water tasted good 'cause we had a deep well in the upper field away from the coal mines.

"It's not nice to call it rotten egg water," she said.

"That's what Cappy called it."

"Well, it's not nice. It's just sulfur in the water. It's not harmful."

One day, Mom filled up a tall bottle with water and I brought it to the playground. Luckily Cappy was there and I gave it to him to taste.

"Sonofabitch, Billy Calvin. You just saved your ass from burning in hell. Jesus, Mary and Joseph, this is goddamn good water."

"It's yours, Cappy. See I told you." Cappy sat on the grounded end of the see-saw and drank the whole thing on that hot afternoon.

"Sonofabitch it's good. You little bastard. You were telling the truth."

"Truth, Justice and the American Way," I said, and Cappy giggled. He was becoming my first friend, though we'd never been inside each other's houses or anything like that. I still liked being alone mostly. But if I saw Cappy on my way to the store or post office I'd stop and talk to him. He always wore a baseball cap, blue with a Spartan soldier's head in the center, and I could spot him the minute I crossed the tracks at the bottom of Tipple Road.

Those summer days were hotter than other summers that I could recall. By the middle of July we had corn and tomatoes in the upper part of the lower field. I had jobs like pulling weeds or picking corn that I liked. Daddy Ray didn't drink. He'd get dressed up and smell good from shaving for the AA meetings. But he didn't sing or play the piano or joke much.

---

anonymous
/əˈnänəməs/

adjective
(of a person) not identified by name; of unknown name.

The AA stood for Alcoholics Anonymous. Anonymous means nobody knows who you are. Some of my poems were by anonymous which was like the person who wrote them was lost or something. I didn't know why the alcoholics were called anonymous, 'cause you could see who they were and you might know their names.

I memorized long poems that summer. *Dangerous Dan McGrew* and *The Cremation of Sam McGee* and *Casey at the Bat.* One day I said *Casey at the Bat* for Cappy.

"Sonofabitch, Billy Calvin, how'd you do that? How'd you get all those rhymin' words?"

"I didn't write it. Ernest Thayer wrote it in 1888. I just memorized it."

"Is that what you learned in first grade?"

"Nah. First grade is just Dick and Jane and Sally and stuff they do like take cookies to their grandmother."

"Where's Mudville anyhow?"

"It's not real. It's just what they call fictional."

"What's fictional?"

"Made up. Ernest Thayer just made it up."

"I like Mudville. You're a smart sonofabitch, Billy Calvin. There is no joy in Mudville," Cappy said.

"I like the somewheres," I said. "I like to think about the somewheres."

"What do you mean?"

"You know, at the end. The somewhere where the sun is shining and another somewhere where the band is playing. And the somewhere where men are laughing."

"Yeah, yeah," Cappy said.

———————

somewhere

/ˈsəmˌ(h)wer/

adverb

in or to some place.

When I'd run into Cappy, he'd ask me to say *Casey at the Bat*. I did *Cremation of Sam McGee* for him and *Dangerous Dan McGrew* but he always wanted to hear *Casey*. I did tell him little fibs about first grade 'cause I didn't want him to be scared. I warned him that you gotta say Miss Parsons 'cause she didn't like Mrs. I tried to make it like she was nice, but I didn't think that was the truth. I hoped second grade would be better; it made my stomach feel tight when I thought about it so I didn't think about it.

Days walk slowly most of the time. Things repeat and a sameness settles into this comfortable repeating so you expect what a day will be and you're right. When you go to bed you breathe easy into your sleep and maybe my sisters say goodnight and maybe I say goodnight. In my bed I hear inside myself. In the pitch blackness of my room I touch a me inside and it rocks me into sleep until another day's sun startles my dreams into forgetting and I'm glad it's another day to walk through.

Cappy couldn't read. I told him he'd learn in school this year. One day at the playground, he had an old *Field and Stream* magazine from when I was just a baby.

"Damn, you're just in time, Billy Calvin. I was wondering what some reading stuff was saying."

"Don't your sisters read to you?" Cappy had two older sisters in junior high. When I first saw them I told my mom they were matching sisters. Everybody laughed when she told that story, which was a lot. I know now they're identical twins and even Cappy isn't always sure which is which.

"Hell no," Cappy said.

Cappy's sisters yelled at him a lot. They'd stand at the top of the bank and yell that he'd better get home now or that his mom said he better not be getting into trouble.

"My sisters used to read to me every night before I learned how to read. Sometimes they still do. It's nice," I said. "What's that you got there? *Field and Stream*."

"What the hell," Cappy said. "*Field and Stream?*"

"That's the name of your magazine. It's like where you'd hunt and where you'd fish. Is it your dad's?"

"Nah, my old man don't hunt or fish. It was just with a bunch of old magazines that someone gave Arlene or Darlene. I like the pictures," Cappy said. "Look at this one. What's it say?"

It was a painted picture of a boy and his dad walking in a hilly field with a red barn in the far distance. The dad was a Dick and Jane father. He wore a hat and he looked at the boy with a big smile. They were both carrying rifles and the artist had painted a gold plate sign at the bottom with the words, 'Jimmie's first gun.'

"What's the reading say?"

"Well, that plaque says: Jimmie's first gun. Below here it says: 'One of the proudest days in any boy's life is the day Dad gives him his first .22 rifle – especially if it's a sturdy Remington with some powerful Remington High-Speed .22 cartridges.' Heck, listen to this. 'We hope that the time is not far off when once again we can supply Remington rifles and shotguns. Today, of course, we are engaged in the production of military supplies.'"

"What's cartridges?"

"That's the bullets."

"Why weren't they making the guns?"

"'Cause of the war. It's an old magazine from before you were born."

"Goddamn, Billy. This reading sure comes in handy."

"Yeah. I love words and reading. Everything about them, except for spelling. At the bottom here, next to the picture of the rifle, those big red letters say, Remington. And in the oval below it, Dupont."

"Sonofabitch. Jimmie's first gun," Cappy said.

"I got a gun like that."

"Don't start your lying lies, Billy Calvin. You'll go to hell and never get out."

"Well it's not mine. But my dad lets me hold it."

"Bullshit. You ain't got no gun, Mr. Liar. I should've wore boots 'cause the bullshit's getting pretty high here."

"Cappy." Arlene or Darlene called from the top bank above the playground. "Cappy, get home."

"Okay," Cappy called.

"Now!" Darlene or Arlene yelled. "Right now!"

"Thanks for doing that reading," Cappy said.

It might have been almost a week later, I did something stupid. Well, Lena said it was stupid and no one corrected her.

The slaughterhouse was done for the day so Daddy Ray could go to an early AA meeting. My mom was in the shop waiting on customers for a couple more hours.

"Hey Mom," I said.

"Hi honey. Close the screen door fast so the flies don't get in. I made chili for dinner. Do you want to eat early with your dad?"

"Nah, I'll wait for later. Can I go to the playground?"

"Sure, but don't be too long."

"I won't."

It wasn't like I planned it or anything. It was just when I started out it came to me. Cappy would probably be at the playground 'cause the guys played ball in the afternoon and Cappy liked to watch them. The slaughterhouse was never locked and the big red sliding door was easy to push. There weren't any windows and the concrete walls made the air cooler with a wet smell that had a faint trace of blood. I switched on the light and pulled over a wooden box so I could reach the rifle hanging in the wall rack. I left the light on and the door slightly open which I shouldn't have.

The rifle felt lighter than I remembered. I cut directly through the corn down to the creek and then crossed the bridge to get to Tipple Road. By the time I reached the end of the flat part, the rifle felt heavy, really heavy. My arm ached from the weight. When I crossed the railroad track, I spotted Cappy's blue baseball cap and I started to run. I shouldn't have ran. I shouldn't have anything about this. The older boys were playing a baseball game and Cappy's sisters and some other girls were sitting under a tree. I don't know where I was when I stumbled and fell. The gun went off but I don't know where I was. Daddy Ray never left a cartridge in the gun. Well almost never, I guess, 'cause the shot rang loud into the hot dust and everybody ran away from the field. Nobody was hit or anything but they all ran, and I ran too, opposite from their running.

I didn't know where I was running to until I was sitting on the bank of the creek, which was the bottom of the steep drop off of Tipple Road near the broken bridge. Dirty sweat ran down my arms and I cradled the rifle, rocking it gently. The ways in which days walk slowly were over. Minutes and hours and days were already running into a blur. But the thing that's weird is that there kept being these ways that in that blur I saw so clear, so very clear. It's hard to explain.

My lungs filled and emptied and I was glad for the cooler air by the creek. The water was higher and moved faster because of the other week's rains. I threw a small branch into its streaming and watched until it got tiny and disappeared but not really. It was just moving on and that moving on was the first thing in the very clear ways. Because I knew the waters moved only in that one direction.

The second thing were these words, large book printed words appeared to me, like I mentioned, very clear. The first word I saw was trouble.

---

trouble
/ˈtrəb(ə)l/

noun

a state or condition of distress, annoyance, or difficulty.

"Billy. Billy Calvin. My name's Officer Kane. Put the rifle down and walk along the creek here. I'll help you up over here at the end of the flat." Officer Kane's voice was both loud and soft, mean and gentle. It seemed to echo off of the creek.

I put the rifle down and walked slowly toward the end of the Tipple Road flat.

"I can climb up myself," I shouted. "I do it all the time."

"Okay, Billy. Okay."

Just as I reached the top where Officer Kane was standing, a siren sound came at me distant, but quickly near and loud and I saw a red light flashing first, just peeking over the ridge of Tipple Road and then the car, up the hill braking onto the flat, loud and red and scary. Then Officer Kane did a strange thing. He held his right hand out, palm to the ground, and pushed down, over and over, pushing the red light out of spinning, pushing the loud siren into the ground, into silence.

"It's okay, Billy," he said. "It's okay." And I thought maybe, maybe it is okay, but then I started to cry. Officer Kane picked me up and just stood there facing the creek. He was tall. I could see the roof of our house over the tops of the trees. I stopped crying and then there was another something about this clear thing. This time it was sort of wide and a feeling, like figuring out a riddle or getting what's funny about a joke. This feeling stayed and made its way into me so that this was the way days would be. It was like my eyes could see things they couldn't see before with the book words hanging in front of me and things wider and faster and in those next weeks and months I never cried again, not once.

Officer Kane put me in the back seat of the car and climbed in beside me. "We're going to drive up to your house. Your mom's waiting for you there," he said, in a whisper, like it was a secret just between him and me.

"The rifle! Wait! The rifle! I have to get my father's rifle back!"

"Sure. Dan, the rifle's at the bottom by the creek. Would you get it? Don't forget your gloves." We sat in silence until the other policeman came back with the rifle.

When we got back to the house Doc Riggle was there. He was very old and very unsmiling, but he seemed kinder and more concerned than when he had come to the house for my measles. My mom hugged me without saying anything and Eleanor and Lena said hey and I said hey.

Doc Riggle handed me a large pink pill. "I want you to take this," he said. "It will make you sleepy and you should take a nap."

I never took naps anymore. I took the pill and swallowed it with a gulp of the water that Lena handed me. I drank all the water and sat at the table in the kitchen. Eleanor came over and wiped at my knee that was dirty with blood. "Ouch," I said, and smiled.

---

custody
/ˈkəstədē/
noun
immediate charge and control, as over a ward or a suspect, exercised by a person or an authority.

Custody was the second word I saw like a sign. It was like the Calvin Provision sign at night, floating in darkness. I didn't know that word but it seemed like a nice thing. It was how Officer Kane left things with Mom.

"We'll leave Billy in your custody tonight. I've scheduled a meeting for eleven o'clock tomorrow at Western." He stopped and glanced at me. "I've written it all down. I won't be there. Captain O'Hara will take over the investigation from here. He'll be there."

"You take that nap, Billy. It'll be okay."

I did feel very sleepy. Mom walked with me up to my room and I lay down on my bed.

"How about if I read to you. I never get to read to you anymore," she said.

"Okay."

"The Teeny Tiny Woman?"

"Nah, that's too baby. But yes, the Teeny Tiny Woman. That's my favorite from when I was little."

"You're still pretty little."

Like lots of the stories when I was little, it starts, "Once Upon a Time." But I was sound asleep before the Teeny-Tiny Woman shouted about the hen.

When I woke up, I wasn't sure if I was awake. Joanne was sitting in a chair beside my bed and I never had a chair in my room and Joanne was away at Grove City.

"How are you doing?"

"Okay," I said. "Sleepy."

"Yeah, that pill will make you sleepy for awhile."

"You're home from Grove City."

"Yes."

"Is it because I'm going to jail?"

"You're not going to jail. I did come to see you because of what you did today."

"The stupid thing."

"Well it wasn't the smartest thing you ever did. But we're not supposed to talk about it before you talk with the counselors tomorrow."

"You mean the police?"

"No. They're just people who want to ask you some questions."

"But."

"We're not supposed to talk about it."

"What's an investigation?"

"It's when they, the police, try to find out what happened."

"Oh."

"It'll be okay," Joanne said.

"That's what Officer Kane said. Look he gave me his card. Is Daddy home yet?"

"No, not yet. He's still at his meeting. There's no place to call him. Are you hungry?"

"No, sleepy."

"You sleep some more."

"Don't go."

"No, I'll be here. You sleep some more."

"It's still light out." I said.

"In winter I get up at night and dress by yellow candle light," Joanne said.

"In summer just the other way," I said. "I have to go to bed by day." We laughed.

I woke up the second time to the sound of the piano and Daddy Ray's voice. The piano was loud and his singing sounded angry. It was that song about Frankie and Johnny and how he had done her wrong. I came down the stairs and sat at a step in the middle, where I could see into the kitchen and through the archway into the living room. I could see Daddy Ray's back, his hands pounding the keys.

Everyone was there, but not around the piano like we sometimes did when Daddy Ray played, but each of us in a separate place. Eleanor was seated on the bottom step. Maria and Lena were at the kitchen table, on opposite ends of the long side. Carolyn was standing, staring out the window behind the piano, and Joanne was sitting on the floor beneath the arch, leaning against the wall, her eyes closed. Bonnie Mom sat next to Dad's piano bench, hugging her knees. We were all there by ourselves. I mean that's weird, I know, but it was like each of us was all alone there in the house, together, but alone.

Daddy Ray's singing growled loud and low: "This story has no moral. This story has no end." But as he came to the final "He done her wrong" it quieted, sweet and soft, draining into silence.

Then we did something kind of strange. We clapped. Leaning in corners, crouched or standing, we clapped. And the clapping seemed to make us one, and not alone and separate. And so we clapped and clapped and clapped.

CHAPTER 11

Wider Days

MOM WOKE ME UP. Usually, as the dreams disappeared into forgotten, the day in front of me rushed to fill my head. Instead the behind me day stayed stuck in my breath, tight and confusing.

I was surprised to see it was already bright morning. Mom had laid out clothes for me to wear, church clothes, except we didn't much go to church anymore, and the day was Wednesday.

"Is this the day we go to talk with the people?"

"Yes. They'll have questions and you should answer them honestly, the best you can."

"Okay."

"You know what you did was very wrong, Billy. No one was hurt, but this is very serious. You do understand that don't you?"

"I guess."

"No, Billy, you must show them that you know that you understand what you did."

"Okay," I said.

"Are you unhappy, honey? Do those boys bully you?"

"No."

Bonnie Mom started to cry. "I'm sorry. I'm not supposed to make you talk about this until . . . I just don't understand."

"Don't cry, Mom. I'll tell them the truth. I always tell the truth."

"I know, I know. Get dressed, honey. I made some oatmeal."

When I came downstairs, Daddy Ray was at the table drinking coffee. He was wearing a suit and a white shirt and a striped tie. Even for the AA meetings he didn't dress in a suit. He stared into the space inside his coffee mug that he cupped between his hands. His eyes squinted in a worry that I usually only saw in my mom's face. When he saw me he switched it off and pushed in a smile to cover it up.

"Looking Spiffy there, Jack."

"You're looking pretty spiffy yourself," I said.

"Well we Calvin men do what we can to not look too shabby around your mom and all those gorgeous Daisy Maes. Dish up some oatmeal. We have to leave by 7 o'clock, so put a nickel in it."

I sat down with my oatmeal and tried to eat like I was hungry. "Dad, I'm sorry I took your rifle and I left the door open and I left the light on."

"Finish your oatmeal, son."

That seemed funny, because Daddy Ray never called me son. Of course I was his son. It made me think of the policeman that woke me up that time that Daddy Ray was in trouble because the Bloody Marys made him drunk. He kept calling me son and of course I wasn't his son.

When Mom came downstairs she was wearing her blue Coco suit that Daddy Ray had bought her as a special, special birthday surprise. We all looked like we were dressed for a special, special something.

———

special

/ˈspeSHəl/

adjective
better, greater, or otherwise different from what is usual.

"Go brush your teeth. Then bring me your toothbrush and I'll put it with the rest of your things. And pick out a couple of books and a few *Jack and Jill* issues to take." Then I saw the small duffle bag she had set on the chair. I had the habit of being silent when I heard or saw things I didn't expect. I needed to think about this. To figure out what my question might be. When I handed Mom my toothbrush and made a wide smile, it was to show I had brushed my teeth. My silence was trying to say; I'll be good, I'll answer the questions, I'll behave.

As we were about to leave, Lena came downstairs. "Good morning, honey," Mom said. "We have to get going. Is everyone still sleeping?"

"Yes," Lena said. "Is Joanne going back to school today?"

"She has to be there for something at 3 o'clock. Carolyn will make dinner. Try to get some more sleep."

"Bye, Billy," Lena said. She gave me an odd kind of hug and came out to the porch in her nightgown. I stared out the back window of the car as we went down the hill and I saw her wave.

It was a long trip. I closed my eyes and it looked like I was sleeping. Daddy Ray and Bonnie Mom whispered but I could hear.

"He doesn't understand, Ray. It seems so silly that we shouldn't talk to him about it."

"He apologized to me for taking my rifle, but also for leaving the light on. Like it was just as bad."

"That's what I mean. And he's so calm. He doesn't understand."

"I don't know about this Western Psychiatric deal. It's like we're already saying there's something wrong and it needs a . . . goddamn, I don't know what? A cure?"

"Officer Kane assured me this was the best solution. It eliminates any judicial review and maybe we just haven't realized what's going on with him," Mom said.

I stirred on purpose because I didn't want to hear anymore. I already needed to remember too many things I never heard of before, like judicial and that sike word. I already knew the word cure from when I had the German measles. But none of it fit in or made sense. I guess I was calm or at least I was still. It was part of the way the world felt so wide open. I needed to be still because everything else was moving so fast.

It was a long drive but then it was there, Pittsburgh. I moved from one side window to the other in the back seat, trying to see everything. Pittsburgh was tall, crowded together buildings, streets everywhere and cars driving on all the streets right and left. The streets had names with little signs on poles. Mom held a map on her lap and watched the little signs telling Daddy Ray to turn left or right. I liked the ones that said one way. Daddy Ray told a joke about a man who explained to a policeman he was only driving one way, but I didn't get it.

"Here it is. Left on Darragh Street," Mom said. Darragh Street was a steep hill. At the top was a huge yellow brick building with a big sign near the roof.

"Western uh," I said, trying to read the sign.

"The P is silent," Mom said.

"Not when you hit the water," I said.

They both laughed and I laughed too. We laughed longer than we needed to because we needed to.

"Psychiatric," Daddy said.

"Okay," I said. I didn't ask the questions I should have, and my silence filled the car.

I had never been in a building with floors on top of floors and elevators to get you up. Both Bonnie Mom and Daddy Ray held my hand. We looked like a family in my Dick and Jane reader. Daddy spoke to the lady at the desk like a radio announcer and when Mom spoke she smiled and filled out papers with her own pen and everyone said good morning and we all acted like we belonged in tall buildings in big cities in our Coco suits with our cheerful good mornings. We took chairs in an empty room called a waiting room and so of course we waited.

A tall woman came in. She had teacher serious looks and a way of talking that said we'll follow her rules this morning, so please listen carefully. Her name was Mrs. Bencloski and she wanted to talk to Mom and Dad without me as soon as Officer O'Hara arrived.

"You must be Billy," she said. I stood up but she sat down in the chair next to me. "I'll talk with your mom and dad, Billy, and then I'll talk with you. How are you doing this morning?"

"Fine," I said.

"How was your trip here?"

"I fell asleep." Just then Officer O'Hara came to the door of the waiting room. Mrs. Bencloski stood. She crossed to him extending her hand in another good morning.

"This is Mr. and Mrs. Calvin and this is Billy. This is Captain O'Hara from your local precinct. He'll be in on our initial interviews."

Daddy Ray shook hands with Captain O'Hara. I didn't know a policeman could be a captain. I knew a poem that started "Oh Captain! my Captain!" but of course a policeman doesn't have a ship.

"Billy, you wait here. There are puzzles there. And books and magazines you can look at. Nurse Linden will be at the desk if you need anything."

Just as they were leaving, Captain O'Hara stopped and turned to me. "How old are you Billy?"

"Six," I said. "But this is my seventh summer."

"Okay," he said. And then he repeated that. "Okay."

●

Our omniscient story might have snapped a picture of that moment, of the adults, crowded at the doorway, glancing back at Billy Calvin, captioned with Captain O'Hara's 'Okay, Okay'. The story with that photo might have started: he was small for his age, which was only six. His feet swung inches above the floor. His blond politeness was punctuated by a half smile. Captain O'Hara hadn't read the news story that appeared in the local paper that morning. But he had read the Associated Press version, the one on the front page of the Pittsburgh Post Gazette. That article, and the stories that grew out of it, created an event with witnesses and motives and precise verbs and adjectives and a beginning and a middle and an end. But Captain O'Hara couldn't match that story with that little boy swinging his legs, pushing his blond hair back from his eyes and trying to muster that half smile in response to those okays. And because it was printed, it was truer than any other story and its explanations got repeated as the once, and the upon, and the time. And though it surrounded Billy Calvin, he never heard that story until he was very old.

○

okay

/ˌōˈkā/

exclamation

used to express assent, agreement, or acceptance.

When everyone left, I dumped a box of puzzle pieces on a low table and knelt beside it. The picture on the box was a small boy with large toys. He held a big toy airplane. A stuffed cow and a bucket were at his feet. Eleanor liked puzzles but I never did. I connected the pieces without thinking, matching the bright colors and creating a larger version of the picture on the box. When I finished, I took out one of the books I brought. Joanne had bought it at a used bookstore near her school. The boy who had owned it had written his name in the front cover and other words in the margins. It was called *My Friend Flicka* and Joanne was surprised I could read it myself. So was Mrs. Bencloski when she came to get me.

"How are you doing here, Billy?" she said.

"Good."

"You put that puzzle together pretty fast. Do you like puzzles?"

"No."

"What are you reading?"

"It's called *My Friend Flicka*."

"Can you read all those words? That's a pretty difficult book you picked out."

"It's my book. I brought it with me." Mrs. Bencloski pulled a chair close to where I was. "Can you read some for me?"

I opened the book and read aloud. I read like a radio man like I did sometimes for Eleanor or Maria. Mrs. Bencloski made notes on her pad.

"Okay, very good, Billy. Let's go into my office. Captain O'Hara is waiting there. Your Mom and Dad went for coffee. They'll be back in a while."

In her office, Mrs. Bencloski had a smaller chair for me to sit in like

100

our desk chairs at school. Captain O'Hara sat beside a big desk. He had a clipboard and papers and he was writing. Mrs. Bencloski sat at the desk and she wrote things.

"You finished first grade this year, Billy. How was school?" Mrs. Bencloski asked.

I remembered that Mom had said to be sure to tell the truth. "I got bad grades," I said. "But I passed."

"Did you like school?" she said.

"No."

"Did you have friends at school?"

"No."

Captain O'Hara had the next question. "Did you play ball with the kids at the playground, Billy?"

"No. Well once or twice, for a bit, but then another player came and they said I couldn't play."

"Was it because you weren't old enough?"

"Danny Pulski's brother played and he was younger than me."

"Why do you think they wouldn't let you play?" Mrs. Bencloski asked.

"Because I dropped the ball when it was hit to me and I couldn't bat to get on base."

"But you did get on base once, and they still said you couldn't play, and you were very upset," Captain O'Hara said. "Did you say they'll be sorry or you'll get even, anything like that?"

"No."

"Were you angry?"

"No, I think I said a promise is a promise, but I wasn't a cry baby."

Mrs. Bencloski was writing things and she said a thing that wasn't a question. "They broke their promise."

It wasn't a question but I said yes because that was exactly right. "It was like a test," I said. "They said if I got on base they'd let me play. I did get on base but they didn't let me play." I didn't know how they knew everything. I thought they might ask if I walked on the train rails or went to the coke ovens over the slate dumps that

101

were off limits. I heard Cappy's voice in my head saying sonofabitch, Billy Calvin, they know how that bread got squished.

"Billy," Captain O'Hara stood up. "Did you plan to take your Dad's rifle to the ball field?"

"How do you mean did I plan?"

----

plan
/plan/

verb
decide on or arrange in advance.

"Did you think about it for awhile?"

"Yes."

"How long would you say you thought about it?"

"Since I saw the Winchester ad in Cappy's old *Field and Stream* magazine."

"How long ago was that?"

"I'm not sure. Before the ears of corn started to come out."

"Thank you, Billy. I'm going to speak with Mrs. Bencloski now. You can go into the waiting room. You're going to stay here at Western. Your mom packed some clothes and things for you to stay here. Do you have any questions?"

"What is psychiatric?"

Mrs. Bencloski answered. "Psychiatry is the study of how people think and feel."

----

psychiatric
/ˌsīkēˈatrik/

adjective
relating to mental illness or its treatment.

"Okay," I said. I got up from my small chair and crossed to Captain O'Hara. I extended my hand and we shook hands like I was a grown up. I smiled and said thank you. I was well behaved. I told the truth. I answered all the questions. I was very well behaved.

CHAPTER 12

Western

WHEN I GOT BACK to the waiting room, Mom and Daddy Ray were there. "It's a good thing they have a waiting room," I said. "You got to do a lot of waiting around here."

"How are you doing, son?" Daddy Ray said. He called me son again.

"Do you mean what's crackin', Jack?" I said. Mom laughed and then she started to cry. "It's okay, Mom," I said. It seemed strange, her crying and me telling her it was okay. "I'm staying here at Western," I said.

"I know, Billy, it will just be for a while."

"Until school?"

"For a while."

"That's good. Tell Lena, the Parcheesi game is under my bed."

"We'll come visit you this Saturday." Daddy Ray rubbed the top of my head then kissed it. He pulled something out of his pocket and put it in mine.

"Your things are in your bag. I gave it to the nurse," Mom said. "I'll bring you more clothes on Saturday. "You'll see Dr. Brenaman this afternoon."

"Am I sick?"

"No."

"Will I get cured?"

"You're not sick, Billy. Just tell the doctors how you feel about things."

"That's what Mrs. Bencloski said. Psychiatric is about how people feel."

"Yes."

Mom hugged me tight and the nurse came in with my bag. She took my hand and Mom and Dad walked with us to the elevators. They didn't get on the elevator with us which was going up even higher. As the elevator door closed Dad took Mom's hand and they both forced a smile like they were having their picture taken. It was like the camera clicked when the doors shut and I kept that photo in a part of my mind like it was in my pocket. This way I wouldn't miss them so much. Now I was out in the world by myself in a big tall building and it wasn't off limits.

I didn't know which feelings I might have to tell about or which things I'd have to figure out how I felt about. I didn't want to tell about my secret places or my favorite words. I knew about feelings. There were lots of feelings in my stories and poems. Like one of my poems, something inside me said, *shh, don't tell.* I loved that poem that Emily wrote. It asked who I was, and if I was nobody too. I liked the idea of being nobody. It connected to being somebody or anybody. It made me think about being, about there or not there like my baby game of peek-a-boo. "*Shh, don't tell,* they'll banish us you know."

---

be

/bē/

verb

exist.

When we stepped off the elevator I said to the nurse, "I guess I'm really banished now." That afternoon, the doctor, Dr. Brenaman who explained he'd be my doctor, knew I said that. It made me think from the start that I was being watched closely, that things were being written down and discussed. That was very different from the busy world of my sisters and Calvin Provision and AA and drinking drunk and getting fixed and arguing and making up, where no one paid close attention to me. Now it seemed my every word would be looked at with a Sherlock

Holmes magnifying glass. I wasn't scared though. It seemed this was just the next thing I had to do, like going to first grade. I knew Mom was right that what I did was very wrong, but I wasn't sure how it was wrong.

We walked down a short hallway and when we got to the place where I would stay she opened the door from the hall with a key. When the door clicked shut behind us, I turned suddenly at the sound. Locked, I thought. Two signs hung large in my mind, one read "in" and the other read "out."

---

locked
/läkt/

verb
to confine or exclude by means of a lock.

Yesterday seemed months away. After I fell and the gun shot, and the policeman came, I thought he'd yell and maybe put me in jail, but he was very nice and now here I was at Western on the eleventh floor.

Western was fine. In those first hours the world in my head kept getting wider and wider. I looked out from the window in the game room. A game room at a psychiatric was one of the things that made it fine. There was even Parcheesi but some of the pieces were missing.

The thing is, even looking out a window, you can do it wrong. When I first looked out, I saw the streets and buildings and a big bridge. Not like the little bridge over Allen Creek, a beautiful huge bridge, far in the distance.

Then the nurse came and said Dr. Brenaman would see me, and that's when he asked me why I thought I was banished, but I said it was just a poem 'cause I didn't really know what banished meant.

---

banish
/ˈbaniSH/

verb
send someone away from a country or place as an official punishment.

105

He also knew about the promise thing with the boys at the baseball field, but I told him I didn't really want to play ball, and I didn't cry about it. He asked me if I was really mad at those boys and I said no and he wrote some things down and said he just wanted to meet me and he'd see me tomorrow, and I smiled and said it was nice to meet him.

I went back to the game room, and that's when I saw how in one way I had looked out the window wrong. Just seeing the streets and the buildings and the bridge in the distance. The thing is, I didn't see right in front of me. I didn't see the bars.

CHAPTER 13

Other Kids Again

I WAS BOUNCING a ping-pong ball on the paddle and I was doing pretty good, when the hall got noisy and then the game room got crowded. It was all boys older than me and bigger. That was silly; I hadn't even thought of that, of course there were other kids here.

The ones that came into the game room mostly eyed me from a distance but some walked up to me and said hello. One boy, Darryl, introduced himself and shook my hand. Another boy came up and said, welcome to the looney bin. His name was Jack. That was funny, a real Jack. I didn't know what a looney bin was. I later learned it was another name for a psychiatric, but not a nice name. A different nurse, Nurse Higgins came into the game room to get me.

"Hey, Miss Higgins, when's lunch?" one boy asked.

"In about a half hour," she said. "Billy, I have your room assignment now. Let me get you settled before lunch."

She took me down the hall and turned into another hall. "This is the dormitory. There are eight beds there, but you're in a single room. We only take fifteen patients on this floor, only boys under twelve years old. There are only twelve patients right now."

"Am I a patient?"

"Yes."

"Am I sick? Because Mom said I wasn't sick."

"No. Not like that. It's a different kind of patient. Here's your room."

It was a tiny closet of a room, like my room in the old house. It was filled up with a bed, a stand with two drawers and a metal lamp on it and another small stand with two drawers.

"You can put your things in these drawers. Lunch is in twenty minutes." She pointed to a small clock on the wall. "Can you tell time?"

"Yes," I said. "It's twenty minutes until noon, which is twelve o'clock."

"Very good. We meet in front of the nurse's station to go down to the cafeteria."

"Thank you Nurse Higgins," I said.

"Oh. Well, you're welcome, Billy," she said.

Lunch was in a cafeteria that was two floors down. I had never been in a cafeteria, but one of the boys, James, showed me how it works, with getting your tray and fork and spoon and how you could pick out what you wanted from the sandwiches and salads and how you told the lady, Mrs. Sanborn, if you wanted soup and also at dinner which thing you wanted like today it could be meatloaf or chicken drumsticks. There were round tables and I sat with James and Darryl and two other boys, Timmy and Sam. Like I said, psychiatric was fine but I still could turn real quick and see in my mind the big signs, the one that said *in* and the other, further and further off that said *out*.

After breakfast the next day, Dr. Brenaman came and got me from the library because it was time to talk to him which I would do every day. But I didn't have to watch the clock or anything because it would be different times and he would come and get me. But if I needed to talk to him, I could ask the nurse and some days and even some nights he could talk to me.

I never was much of a talker. I loved words but I didn't like to talk them, except my memorized poems which Maria said was amazing how I did that with *Casey*, and *Dangerous Dan*, and *Sam McGee*. Lots of times someone, usually Carolyn, would tell that story of how I said a whole poem when I was only two but that wasn't really true.

Dr. Brenaman asked questions about things he knew and I didn't know how he could know so many things, but of course he talked to Bonnie Mom and Daddy Ray.

"Billy, do you remember when your dad locked you in the car and went drinking and the police found you?"

"Yes."

"How did you feel?"

"I don't know."

"Were you scared or angry?"

"No."

"What happened when the police located your father?"

"They took us to the police station and my mother came."

"And you were very upset when she got there. Do you remember?"

"Sort of."

"Did you ever ask your father why he did that?"

"No."

"What would you say to him now, if you were to tell him how you felt?"

"I'd say I'm sorry."

"Why would you be sorry?"

"For getting him in trouble."

"How did you get him in trouble?"

"Because the policeman saw me in the car. But I wasn't crying. I'm not a crybaby."

"No, Billy. I didn't mean you were a crybaby. But, how was it your fault?"

"I don't know."

"Did you think you were to blame for your father getting arrested?"

"Yes. Well, not to blame, just like cause and effect. In the *Junior Instructor* book there's a science reading about cause and effect. I was the cause and Daddy Ray getting arrested was the effect. But I definitely wasn't a crybaby. But I would say to Daddy Ray, I'm sorry. Except I never did."

"We'll talk again tomorrow, Billy."

CHAPTER 14

Therapy

EVERYTHING was a therapy. It was one of the words that hung in the air like a sign. But I didn't know what it meant.

———

therapy
/ˈTHerəpē/

noun
the treatment of mental or psychological disorders by psychological means.

There was occupational therapy which was just like art but you could make things out of clay and they'd get put in an oven and be like a real ash tray or bowl. Physical therapy was just games on a basketball court and group therapy was just talking with five other of the younger kids but I was the youngest.

Library was my favorite, but it wasn't really a therapy. I had never been in a library. My town didn't have one and my school didn't either. But I knew from the *Junior Instructor* book what a library was. It's lots of books and you can find them real easy because they are put on shelves in letter order and in categories like true or fictional or poems. At this library you can check books out with your name on a card and take it with you for a couple of weeks. If you didn't finish it you could check it out again.

It was Jack who started calling me Brainy. But it stuck with the other kids and became my nickname. I didn't know what it meant but it was because I read books all the time. Jack liked me 'cause when I saw him I'd say, "What's crackin', Jack?" Like Daddy Ray always said to me. Jack was always nice to me, but not to other kids and he'd be put in a special room because he might have hit someone or tripped them.

There were other people on all different floors but we only saw them sometimes in a line. It was just us at lunch or library or therapies so we stuck together and helped each other. I always got to play in physical therapy and if Jack was captain, he always picked me first if there was pick-up but usually it was count off for kickball or basketball or dodge-ball where you had to dodge which means get out of the way so the ball didn't hit you. If another kid threw it real hard at me, Jack would push him, and I felt bad 'cause then he'd be put in that special room.

"What's crackin', Jack?" I said one morning. It was just him in the game room.

"Hey Brainy, how's things going?"

"Pretty good, so far."

"Well you can only go so far around here, 'cause it's all locked up."

"Yep. And we're in and out is out." Jack liked that. He laughed and laughed.

"Yep. Out is definitely out."

"Hey, Jack. Don't get in trouble for me, okay. I can dodge good. Besides, you don't want to be put in the room."

"You're my main man, and I explained real nice that they shouldn't be messin' with you. Real nice."

"Well, thanks." A man I didn't know, dressed in a suit and tie, came into the game room.

"What's up Doc?" Jack said.

"Good morning, Jack. Are you ready for our talk?"

"You're the talk doc. So I'm ready. See you later Brainy."

Dr. Brenaman saw me nearly every day, but he wasn't that much of a talk doc at first. It was just a bunch of testing. Not like tests in school, but words I had to put with pictures and funny shapes I had to say what I could make up about them. But then one day he picked me up at the library and started right off with talking when we got to his office.

"Do you know why you're here, Billy?"

"Because the door's locked," I said.

That was a joke. But Dr. Brenaman didn't laugh or even smile. He didn't do either one very often.

"Do you understand what you did wrong?"

"I took my dad's rifle and left the door open and the light on."

"Do you hate anyone, Billy?"

"No. Mom and Dad don't allow us to even use that word. Eleanor had to go to her room just for saying that about a boy in her class."

"What feelings would someone have if they hated someone?"

"I guess mad, pushing feelings, dangerous maybe, like Dan McGrew."

"Who is Dan McGrew?"

"He's fictional, in a big long poem I know."

"What's it about?"

"It's about Dan McGrew and a stranger who maybe stole his gold and they shot each other when the lights went out."

"And you like the poem?"

"Oh yeah. Casey, and Sam McGee, and Dan McGrew are my favorite big poems. I like lots of little ones too. I like poetry which is poems, but also stories and long stories which are novels."

"What's that book you have with you?"

"A book from the library called *Cheaper by the Dozen*, and then some poems by Robert Frost. We can take two books out for two weeks, but I checked out Robert Frost before. How long have I been in here?"

"Sixteen days."

"My mom and dad visited me twice. But I miss my sisters and my house and my favorite places."

"What are your favorite places?"

"Just places I like to go." I didn't want to tell about my favorite places because they were secret. I shouldn't have mentioned them.

"Like the slaughterhouse?"

"No."

Dr. Brenaman wrote things down and just waited.

"I miss my sisters. When can I go home?" I said.

"Well, I think that Carolyn and Maria could visit. I'll tell your mom and dad about that. Joanne too, but I understand she has school and a job. Lena and Eleanor are too young. That's all for today, Billy. I'm going away to a conference so I won't see you until next Thursday."

"Thank you, Dr. Brenaman."

I didn't know how he knew all my sisters and even what Joanne did. And how could Lena and Eleanor be too young to even visit, if I wasn't too young to be here? I didn't like all this looking at me, and no place to be alone except my room, which was mostly off limits during the day unless you told Nurse Higgins you didn't feel good or something. I went to the nurse's station and asked Nurse Higgins if I could lie down for a bit because I didn't feel so good and she said yes.

●

After Billy Calvin closes the door, the omniscient story remains in the now dimly lit office. Dr. Brenaman has turned the lights off and the angled sun casts shadows across the small space. He has removed the brace he wears on his left leg because of the paralysis from childhood polio. He is already a distinguished expert in child psychology and is formulating another phase of his theories on repression, based on the writings of Sigmund Freud. Freud wrote: "Repression develops under the influences of the superego and the internalized feelings of anxiety in ways leading to behavior that is illogical, self-destructive or antisocial." Dr. Brenaman's newest patient, William Calvin, a six-year-old boy who tried to shoot the boys who excluded him from their games, was a prime example for the extension of these theories. This patient exhibited no hostility, no anger, almost no emotion. He made a note in the margins of the paper he would be presenting at the coming conference:

The case of William Calvin appears to be an example of how repressed emotions can lead to highly aggressive actions that are then repressed.

He rubbed his leg. He was used to the persistent pain but it often drained his energy when he needed most to be at his best.

○

I must have fallen asleep because when I awoke, I realized it was already past the time for occupational therapy. Nurse Higgins was at the desk beside the files and chairs they called the nurse's station, but it wasn't really a station.

"Did everyone go to occupational therapy?"

"Yes, Billy. This is Thursday."

"But I'm supposed to get my bowl back from the oven."

"Oh. Well, how about if I call down for Tom and see if he can come up for you."

Tom was one of the orderlies. He was the nicest one. Alvin who was here at night sometimes yelled, but Tom never did. An orderly keeps things orderly by reminding us of the rules. Tom was huge, tall, even taller than Daddy Ray and well, while I'm not supposed to call people fat, Tom was fat. His skin was almost the color of coal which made his teeth look very white when he smiled and he smiled all the time.

In just a few minutes, Tom was there. "Hey Brainy, wait until you see your bowl," he said. He took my hand as we walked to the elevator. "Do you remember what color you picked for your bowl?"

"It was supposed to be blue but it just looked muddy grey when I painted it."

"Wait until you see it," he said again. Of course I had to wait to see it until the elevator took us to the occupational therapy rooms. But Tom's saying didn't mean wait. It meant you're going to be surprised and in a good way. And boy was I surprised. Miss Langley had put my bowl on a tall table with a tiny top called a pedestal. It was blue, shiny and deep blue. The mud grey had turned into a mirror of blueness. The curves I had made with my fingers at the top of the bowl were like petals or leaves or the pieces of a puzzle that were part of the no cloud sky.

"It's so blue beautiful," I said.

Tom was looking at me with a never stop smile. "I told you, he said. "I told you." I went to Tom and gave him a tight hug which only reached around his knees and everyone laughed.

CHAPTER 15

Visitor's Day

THE NEXT VISITOR'S DAY I gave the blue bowl to Mom and she couldn't believe I made it. I didn't like visitor's day. I liked it for me. I'd get to see Bonnie Mom and Daddy Ray. Dr. Brenaman did fix it so Maria and Carolyn came with Mom one time and one time Joanne met Mom and Dad here. But I didn't like it because a lot of kids were really upset after and some of them had to see their doctors or get a pill. I didn't get any pills ever. We visited in a bunch of small rooms on the fourth floor. That was the lowest floor we ever went to except once a month when we went out of the building to go to a swimming pool at the college school.

Visitor's day was every week and always on a Saturday. Some kids could go out with their families to lunch or for a walk. But I couldn't yet. There were lots of "not yets" at psychiatric, but I was good at waiting.

---

yet
/yet/

adverb
up until the present or a specified or implied time;
by now or then.

When I got to the visitors room, it was just Joanne. I ran to her and hugged her for a long time, because I was feeling lots of feelings but I didn't cry or anything. "Where's Mom and Dad?" I said.

"Well, they couldn't come today. Mom's helping in the shop and Daddy, oh darn; I'm not going to lie to you. Daddy is drinking again."

"I thought he was anonymous."

"Well he's still in AA and some of the other men came to talk to him. But you know Daddy, when he starts drinking, he does nothing but drink for weeks and won't get help until he's ready."

"No, I didn't know."

"You shouldn't worry about that. I shouldn't have told you."

"No. You should. Truth, Justice and the American Way."

"Superman."

"Did you come here from school, or were you home?"

"I drove down from Grove City. Look, I brought you something. It's from that used book store I love. I know you have this poem in another book, but look at this edition. It's just this one poem, 'The Cremation of Sam McGee', but the illustrations are great."

"Illustrations are the pictures. Right?"

"Yes."

"I love it. Thank you, Joanne. Look, he's building a big fire to cremate Sam."

"It's a little spooky," Joanne said.

"Yeah, but it's funny too 'cause Sam says it's the first time he's been warm since he left Tennessee."

"You know all the details," Joanne said.

"I know the whole poem by heart. I know lots of poems by heart."

"You're amazing." Joanne pulled me toward her and kissed my cheek. Tears came to her eyes. "Are you okay here, honey?"

"Sure, psychiatric's fine. But I have to go home real soon 'cause school's going to start."

"Well, I think you'll get a tutor here. That's what Dr. Brenaman told Mom. You will be with a boy named James. Do you know James?"

"Sure. James is my real good friend. Then I don't have to go to school?"

"Well don't be so sad about it," Joanne said. That was a joke 'cause I couldn't hide that I was glad about not going back to my school.

"Did you really not like school? You're so smart."

"No. I almost didn't pass."

"That's weird. Did you hear that Carolyn got a really good job as a pediatric nurse at Westmoreland Hospital?"

"That's great. What's pediatric?"

"Children. She'll be a nurse for little kids."

"Would I be a pediatric?"

"Yes. Sure. It's a specialty because adult medicine is different from children's medicine."

"There are only kids on my floor."

"This is one of the best hospitals in the United States."

"Am I in a hospital? I thought this was a psychiatric."

"No, I mean yes. I shouldn't have said that."

"It's like a jail. Jack said it's like a jail."

"That's not true."

"The doors are locked and the windows have bars."

"Billy, it's not a jail."

"But is it a hospital? Am I sick?"

"No. It's a place to help you. Look at all the things you do. And you're doing great. The nurses I talk to say you're doing really great."

"Psychiatric is fine. It's fine. And I'm glad to get a tutor instead of going to school. What's a tutor?"

"It's your own teacher, just for you and James."

"Good."

"I brought cards," Joanne said. "Do you want to play Fish?"

"Sure."

Joanne dealt the cards. "Do you have any threes?" she said.

"Go fish," I said.

CHAPTER 16

Group Therapy

WHEN JOANNE LEFT, I wanted to cry, but somehow I couldn't. I'm not a crybaby, but I wanted to cry. I needed to let go of these feelings that surrounded me more and more in psychiatric. It was part of being looked at and questioned and things written down. Not just my answers, but maybe the answers about my answers. But I didn't know what that might be. I really, really missed being outside, being by myself. I would stare out the window at the beautiful bridges and all the streets that each had their own name, with little signs. But I couldn't read the signs or walk across the bridges or smell the air or see the stars. It's like I was still on Earth, one of my always favorite places, but I couldn't touch it.

Joanne said she shouldn't have mentioned that psychiatric was a hospital and Mom said I wasn't sick. Maybe Jack was right, that this was just another kind of jail that policeman could put you in if you were too little to go to a regular jail. But what about all the nice things like the cafeteria and the library. The other kids were my friends now, and I had never had friends except sometimes when I saw Cappy.

I was glad I wouldn't have to go to my school and that I would just be in a tutor with James. But school was the line in front of me that when I crossed it, I would go home. Now I didn't know when I would go home. I behaved all the time. I never got into fights or had to be put in the room.

If this was a hospital and if I was sick, I couldn't help thinking about how I would feel when they got done curing me.

Everyone was mostly quiet at dinner even though it was spaghetti and meatballs, which was everyone's favorite and usually made us laugh and talk.

"There's something in the air," James said. He was twirling his spaghetti on a fork and wouldn't bite it until it was wound up perfectly.

"What's in the air?" I said.

"It's just an expression."

"It's visitor's day. It did it to me too this time," I said.

"I didn't have a visitor," Paul said. "I talked to my mom on the phone. She said she was sick."

"Jack said the looney tunes were all out of tune today," Frank said. We all had a short laugh about that.

We didn't have assigned tables for meals, but Paul and James and Frank and I always sat together. Sometimes Arnie sat with us. Arnie never talked. I mean I never heard him talk. Arnie was another kid that Jack always watched over like he did for me. Arnie would sometimes bang his head on the wall or floor and Jack would hold his arms to stop him, rocking him slowly until he was calm so no one had to call the nurse.

That evening, Arnie did the head banging thing on the game room floor. Jack wasn't there, and Alvin, the orderly on duty, was in the lounge. By the time James, who was playing checkers with me, ran to get Nurse Lane and Alvin, his head was bleeding a whole lot. I think he ended up in the infirmary where you went if you got injured and especially if you were contagious, which means any one could catch your sickness.

If James was right at dinner that there was something in the air, now that something hung thick. It was like the hurting was contagious and we were all coming down with it. What if we too had to bang our heads again and again until the sadness bled out of us?

That next Thursday, Arnie was back in group, but like I said, he never talked. Group therapy was every Tuesday and Thursday with Dr.

Miller who was young and never wore a tie and would sometimes play the guitar in the library for us.

"What's happening in the group?" Dr. Miller said. We all laughed, soft and uneasy like, because that's how Dr. Miller started every group meeting which went for an hour or so. Then he'd just wait silently until someone spoke up about something.

"They should tell us about getting out," Daryl said. "We never know how much longer we have to be here." Maybe he said that because Arthur was discharged on Wednesday which means he went home. Now our group was just the five of us. Me and Arnie, Daryl, James and Jerry. We were the youngest kids on the floor. Jerry reminded me of Cappy because he always swore. The nurses and orderlies would tell him not to but Dr. Miller never did.

"Sonofabitch if I can tell how that crazy bastard Arthur got out. Like he got sane. Hell, probably his rich daddy paid to get him out."

"Arthur was my friend in the dormitory," James said. "I'll miss him, but it's good to get to go home. I'm going home to visit for three days, but it's just a trial."

"I thought a trial was when they arrested you and the judge or jury said you were guilty or not," I said.

"That's one kind of trial," Dr. Miller said. "James' trial is just some time at home to see how it goes."

"I'm not so depressed these days," James said.

"I was supposed to go home so I could go to school," I said. "But now I'm going to tutor school here instead."

"How do you feel about that?" Dr. Miller said.

"It's good," I said. "I didn't like school."

"Hell, I forgot about that," Jerry said. "Damn that is a good thing. No school."

Dr. Miller never wrote things, which I liked. Even the nurses sometimes wrote things. It was like they were figuring us out. Sherlock Holmes would explain a case to Watson and tell him how the clues fit together. It seemed like they were all writing down clues and trying to solve the case that would be James or Daryl or Arnie or me.

"Since I'm not so depressed," James said. "maybe they'll send me home."

"How do you feel about going home?" Dr. Miller said.

"It makes me depressed," James said. We all laughed.

"I hate school," Arnie said. We all turned and looked at Arnie. None of us had ever heard him speak before. Although that was all he said and then he didn't talk.

"Me too," Daryl said. He went to Arnie and shook his hand.

When the session was over and we were walking out, Jerry put his arm around Arnie. "Sonofabitch, it's a good thing Brainy reminded us that at least we're not in school." Arnie never said another word, but he smiled.

There was something big that happened between us that day in group therapy. We always shrugged off those sessions with Dr. Miller, joking about him in the game room or in the middle of a dodgeball game, one of us saying, "Hey what's happening in the group?" But I began to think that what was happening in the group was really happening. Not just in one day or in one way, but in this thing that slowly landed between us, that was not the me or the I or the you, those earliest baby words that separated us into our aloneness in the world, but a happening between us that we all felt when the feeling was so stopped that you might bang your head to find anything to replace the nothing.

That night after there was lights out, I lay awake a really long time. I kept thinking about feelings and which words I didn't know that let feelings get away with no naming. Dr. Brenaman, my talk doc, was big on naming those feelings. But I didn't know so many words; even though I loved words and read them and tracked them down to find out what they meant. But what if the word was in French or Dutch, in ways of talking I didn't know at all.

opposite

/ˈäpəzət/

adjective

contrary to one another or to a thing specified.
being the other of a pair that are corresponding.

I lay there thinking about my favorite word for thinking these days, the word *opposite*. Probably because of the opposite signs that hung in the air, *in* and *out*, which were everything about psychiatric where I was in and not out. Today the group was feeling a lot about that in and out. What if we were out and not in, like going home and how in some ways that was scary too. But I missed home, and now I wasn't sure how long I had been here or how long I'd have to stay.

As I got sleepy, opposite words whirled around me: dark and light, true and false, above and below, afraid and brave, right and wrong. My old favorites: before and after, alike and different, always and never, asleep and awake. And then it was thinking, and then it was dreaming.

CHAPTER 17

Counting Time

SOMEWHERE near the psychiatric there was a clock that sounded its chimes, counting the quarter hour, the half hour, the hour. Some kids didn't like it, but I did. Although really, visitor's day was the only time counter that said hours of being here had chimed into another week. Someone always came to see me. In the weeks after Joanne told me Daddy Ray was drinking, only Maria and Carolyn came once. Another time Carolyn came with Mom. Bonnie Mom came by herself once by train and taxi because she didn't drive but she was studying how to drive and would be taking a test.

On visitor's day, the nurse or the orderly would let you know you had a visitor and you would go to the nurses' station and someone would take us all down to the fourth floor. You never knew who your visitors were until you got there. We were always silent and slightly shy waiting for the elevator, which was unusual. I saw Jack lining up and was glad because Jack almost never had a visitor, mainly 'cause he was from Delaware but maybe other reasons too.

"What's crackin', Jack?" I said.

"Guess I got a visit from the governor," he said.

"The governor?"

"Sure. I think he's come to pardon me. Spring me out of this joint."

Jack liked to joke a lot so I just laughed though a lot of times I didn't get the joke.

When I got to the private room where my visitor would be, I saw it was Daddy Ray by himself. He hugged me.

"I haven't seen you in a while," I said.

"I know. It's been real busy. You know making that sausage, ha ha. But business is great. Has almost doubled from this time a year ago. This is our busiest time of the year anyhow. Farmers want their stock custom dressed at the end of the summer. I've been breaking in a new guy, but he's not really up to speed yet."

Daddy Ray never talked so much. I guess lies take more talking than truth. I just said things like that's good news or maybe I just said good. But the lies felt like stones in a wall and my smile started to make my head ache. I started thinking how words like dressed or stock or even the company name, Calvin Provision, never mentioned cows or killing or slaughterhouse and I was wondering how words can lie by themselves even if their sentence is telling the truth. But then Daddy Ray had a surprise.

"Guess what?" he said. "We got permission to go out to lunch."

"Wow. Now?"

"Nurse Higgins is bringing a paper we'll need for the front desk. In a few minutes, I think."

Nurse Higgins dropped off that paper and said we had an hour or so. I felt nervous and I didn't know why.

Outside the air was cool, but the sun felt warm and then hot. "See that building," I said. "They take us swimming there once a month. How long have I been here?"

"A little over six weeks."

"Because I've only been swimming once. I already learned to float. James called it the dead man's float 'cause you don't move. I'm going to be tutored with James starting Monday."

"That's what I heard."

We walked silently down the steep hill they called Darragh Street and turned left on Forbes which was an avenue which means it's a big street or maybe it runs in a different direction. Like I probably mentioned, I almost more than anything missed being outside and being alone. In Pittsburgh you probably couldn't find alone places very easily. People didn't know you like they did in Arona so I guess it might be the same as being alone. The lunch place was crowded so we had to sit at the counter. I liked that 'cause it reminded me of the place at the auction where I got pie and coffee. "This is like Mike's counter at 84 Auction," I said. Not just the auction, but the town was named that number.

"I started going to a really big auction across the border in West Virginia. I'll take you with me when you come home."

"When?"

"When you come home."

"When will that be?"

"I don't know, Jack. It's not up to me. But they tell me you're doing good, real good, so it shouldn't be too long, and we'll go to that auction, the big one in West Virginia."

●

Ray Calvin got drunk on his very first trip to that auction in West Virginia. He had loaded the full limit of livestock onto his truck and headed home. After crossing the border into Pennsylvania, he stopped at a roadside bar with a flashing neon that read 'Lucky's'. It wasn't lucky. He ran the truck off the road into a ravine. When he called his wife, Bonnie, she agreed to send Carl and Tony, two of their workers to get him. She phoned 84 Auction and got the name of an independent trucker who hauled cattle and Carl and Tony took charge of transferring the livestock onto the other truck. By the time a State Trooper stopped to check on what was happening, Ray Calvin was sleeping in the back of Tony's station wagon. Carl explained that he had miscalculated the edge of the pull off. Just then a tow truck that Bonnie Calvin had arranged for arrived to tow the empty truck back onto the road. Carl drove the cattle truck that only had minor damage to the right fender and Tony drove his station wagon with Ray Calvin asleep in the back seat.

Bonnie Calvin clipped the names and phone numbers her efficiency had garnered in a neat pile and placed them in the junk drawer of a kitchen cabinet. They called it a junk drawer but it was neat and orderly with rubber bands, pens, note pads, coupons, green stamps, and a phone directory, each in a designated place. She made a fresh pot of coffee in the commercial coffee maker she used daily. Two men from Ray Calvin's AA group were coming over. She knew that since Ray had just started drinking, the men from AA were unlikely to convince him to stop, but their presence was one of her measures, part of her order. She relaxed easily into emergencies or urgencies, measured them, solved them and while she wouldn't admit it, enjoyed them. She announced the situation to each of her daughters in the same exact way: "Your father's drinking." Nothing more was ever said about it. There was disappointment, anger, frustration but these were only fuel to a comfortable efficiency that clicked into gear every time Ray Calvin went on a binge, fell off the wagon, began drinking the bar pour whiskey that moved him quickly through a brief euphoria to a darkness that held no comradery, no song, no jokes, no laughter, no love, or lust or light.

Bonnie took the phone from the stand by the staircase and placed it on the end of the long kitchen table. She poured herself a cup of the fresh coffee and sat down. Her short black hair was pushed back behind her ears. This was always a signal to her family that something was wrong. She had to call her oldest daughter Joanne. She sometimes didn't tell Joanne her father was drinking because she came home infrequently enough that she could avoid worrying her, and she did worry. But she had to arrange for Joanne to visit her youngest child, Billy, who was in a psychiatric facility in Pittsburgh. Billy's was the situation she couldn't control and she choked back tears and dialed the phone. She made sure that a Saturday visiting day didn't go by without someone in the family being there.

Because Bonnie Calvin made sure of things, arranged things, ran things, it allowed Ray Calvin to drink into that darkness for a week or two or sometimes three before he pleaded to be sent to Bethel's in Milford Ohio. He would beg to be eased out of the approaching delirium tremens into a tenuous sobriety. Bethel's inpatient alcohol rehab program was expensive, even though the methods in 1949 were little more than confinement for seven to ten days and paraldehyde. But Bonnie kept the business running, even growing, and money wasn't an issue. With the help of AA meetings Ray Calvin would stay sober for four or five or even six months before his wife would announce without emotion, your father's drinking.

○

Daddy Ray and I sat in silence. It was a silence we were used to but I was glad when our grilled cheese with tomato sandwiches came. It was good to eat and we both relaxed a bit. Daddy Ray told me a riddle I couldn't guess.

"What always runs, but never walks, often murmurs, never talks, has a bed but never sleeps, has a mouth but never eats?"

"I don't know."

"A river."

"That's a good one," I said. Daddy Ray was surprised when I repeated it exactly.

"I can see a river from my room," I said.

"You can?"

"And a beautiful bridge that crosses it, with huge arches," I said. I never mentioned about the bars on my window because Daddy Ray and I were having a nice time.

CHAPTER 18

Learn

TUTORING WITH JAMES was great. John Gibbon was our teacher and he said we could just call him John. Tutoring was in the library but John had other books that we had to study and worksheets and a slide projector that were all his different lessons. James was ahead of me. He would be in third grade at his other school and I would only be going to second. John gave us standard tests to start so he could see what we already knew. We had lessons for four hours, four days a week plus we had homework, but of course we never went home.

At first I felt bad being glad that James was my school partner because it meant his home trial didn't go that good. It turns out he was guilty. Not like a judge says you're guilty but James said he felt guilty because he was happy he wasn't going home but then the happy part made him feel guilty, which was a word that confused me with judges and juries and feelings.

---

guilty
/ˈgiltē/

adjective
culpable of or responsible for a specified wrongdoing.
ashamed or affected by a feeling of guilt.

John switched both our arithmetic books after he saw our standard test answers. James went ahead two grades and I went back one grade.

I began using the dice Daddy Ray had given me to practice adding and subtracting. I showed John how I did it so that he could see I was practicing a lot.

"So I throw the dice and let me see. I got a five and a six. So five plus six is eleven and also six plus five is eleven."

"Yes, that's the commutative property," John said. "The position of the numbers doesn't affect the answer. Addition has that property but subtraction does not."

"What's a property?"

"It's a quality that something has. Color or weight are properties of objects."

---

commutative

/ˈkämyəˌtādiv, kəˈmyo͞odədiv/

adjective

a property in arithmetic that states: the order of the numbers in addition do not change the sum.

I threw the dice again. "For subtraction," I said. "Five minus two is three and three minus five, well you can't do that."

James who was doing worksheet problems at another table came over to us. "Yes you can. It would be minus two or negative two," he said.

"That's right," John said. "But Billy's not ready for that yet."

"Well, it would be like when it's really freezing out," I said. "and it gets to be like three below or something."

"Excellent," John said.

"Good thinking, Brainy," James said. "Of course negative two and positive two are different numbers."

"So that's why subtraction doesn't have the commutative property," I said.

"Exactly. You guys are thinking in the fast lane." John was smiling and then laughing. "But get to work on your own problems, James."

When John gave arithmetic reasons and words, I began to really like it. John explained everything and we learned and learned. It made us giggly, this speed of learning. It was like a sled ride and sometimes it took my breath away. I was good at it too, especially reading and memorizing. Because I was good with words, I liked that arithmetic had things like properties and positive and negative numbers. John explained that the history of numbers told us about the people who first thought of these things, some parts thousands of years ago, and that was called mathematics, which was arithmetic and other stuff like geometry and algebra which I would learn later. I said that I wished I could think so hard that I would think of something first before anybody and John said I might and James might too.

One day John had a globe which was a miniature Earth with all the place names. He pointed to the tiny dot where we were in Pittsburgh. "In Pennsylvania," John said. "In the United States, in North America, on the Earth." He picked up the globe and moved around the table. "In the solar system, in the Milky Way Galaxy." I told John and James that Earth was one of my favorite secret places.

"How can the whole Earth be a secret place?" James said.

"Where I live, I can be in the lower meadow or the back field by the stream and you can't see any houses or people and if you stare up at the sky you feel like it's just you and the only connection to a place with a name is Earth. When I first learned about Earth, I felt that connection was my secret."

"I like that," John said and James agreed.

I walked over to the library windows to release a breath that I was holding tight. I guess I just told a feeling, and my next breath felt deep and easy.

It turns out it's all connected together, this learning stuff. The mathematics and history and geography and science and reading and writing. I practiced my printing all the time. I could think of a favorite word and I could print it down and then print other words it made me think of.

I could print poems from memory onto the page so anyone could read it. I printed the Emily poem about being nobody and gave it to James. He thanked me and hugged me and said I was his best friend. It was great having friends at psychiatric and a best one like James.

I learned other stuff too. Like when we went to the pool the second time I learned to move from floating to swimming. Jack was a good swimmer and he helped me with tips like how to think about breathing which really was good because whoever would think to think about breathing.

---

tip
/tip/

noun
1. a small but useful piece of practical advice.
2. a sum of money given to someone as a reward for their services.

verb
overbalance or cause to overbalance so as to fall or turn over.

I liked little words like tip that had lots of meanings. The kind of tip that Jack had given me at swimming was the helpful hint kind. My tutor, John, had given me a dictionary because my spelling was so bad. Although he worked with me a lot on spelling and made me look up words that I couldn't spell, he never tested me on lists or said anything mean about my wrong spelling. The other neat thing about looking up words was that it told you its history. The word tip is over five hundred years old. Like I said, it turns out all this learning is connected. And then you start to see how learning doesn't just happen in lessons or even just in reading, but can happen anywhere, like in the swimming pool when Jack gave me that tip.

Since tutoring started for everyone, there were two hours of quiet time after dinner to do our homework. We still had some free time on the floor or in the library. If we went to the gym in the evening, the game was picked by the nurse or orderlies, so the time wasn't really free.

One Thursday, Nurse Higgins announced that we would be reporting to the gym. Reporting was just the same as going, but it was another way of saying you didn't have a choice.

---

choice
/CHois/

noun
an act of choosing between two or more possibilities.

In some ways, psychiatric was like being in school all the time because you did things when you were told to. I liked the things we did but one of the feelings that kept getting stronger, although I didn't mention it to anyone, was wanting to go home. Of course I didn't have a choice.

Anytime we were reporting somewhere we first gathered at the nurse's station. Tom was on duty. He and Nurse Higgins and Nurse Hale were going down to the gym with us.

"I think maybe," James said.

"Maybe what?" I said.

"You'll see."

When we got there, the gym floor was lined with folding chairs and everyone got really excited. In front of the chairs was a white sheet stretched tight between two poles.

"What's that machine?" I asked James.

"That's the projector. I was right; we're going to see a movie."

"I've never seen a movie," I said.

"Never?"

"No."

"Well you're going to love it, Brainy."

Nurse Higgins explained some rules: no talking or standing up from your seats and no putting your hand in front of the projector light. We could clap, she said, and everyone did even though the movie hadn't even started. She announced that the name of the movie was *National*

Velvet and everyone clapped again. A bright light shined the movie onto the white sheet called a screen and a lion roared and everyone clapped some more.

James was right. I loved it. The words on the screen read, "A long time ago in a spinning world." And then the spinning world was alive. The people seemed almost real and the story about a girl named Velvet who loved a wild horse, had everyone silent. She named the horse The Pie. She wanted to race The Pie in the Grand National, the toughest race in the world with huge jumps and twists and turns. First they had to train, which was practicing and practicing for months.

I liked the older boy played by Mickey Rooney who helped Velvet train The Pie for the big race. He had been a jockey and he wasn't always good, but in the end the good won out over the bad. In one part of the movie we saw him go from not drunk to drunk and it made me think of Daddy Ray.

Velvet's mom, it turns out, had prize money she had saved from swimming the English Channel and she gives it to Velvet for the entrance fees and jockey pay. I guess in the movies things go from good, to bad, to good, really fast.

Then it was bad again because they couldn't find a jockey. So, Velvet cut her hair and put on the jockey clothes 'cause she had practiced with The Pie and so she decided to be the jockey. By the time the race was ready to start, we were all leaning into the screen, hoping Velvet wouldn't be spotted; hoping she wouldn't get hurt, hoping like it all was real. Everyone clapped and cheered during the race. I always loved stories in books. But with the movie stories, we all laughed at the same time or were surprised at the same time. We were all doing the hoping together and by the end of the race, when Velvet was first across the finish line, we couldn't even follow the rule about staying seated and we were on our feet clapping and yelling, even Tom and the nurses, even Arnie. It wasn't like the alone in a book story. It was a wonderful kind of together.

Velvet didn't get the prize money because of a rule about not falling off your horse, even after you cross the finish line which had everyone hushed again but still it all turned out good, like my earliest stories with their happy every after.

That night, in my bed, after lights out, I kept thinking about how together we were in this spinning world, like the words read at the start of the movie. I thought of John's globe in our geography lesson, spinning so fast with me on it and everyone I knew on it and everyone I didn't know on it. Spinning and spinning.

CHAPTER 19

Talk Doc

DR. BRENAMAN was nice, even if he didn't smile a lot. I told him he was the talk doc, Jack's name for the different doctors each of us see alone. He didn't laugh or smile. He just asked me another question about Daddy Ray's drinking. He seemed to know a lot about stuff. He mostly asked me about these things he knew, so I never told him much about the things he didn't know.

"Did your mother and father have arguments about your father's drinking?"

"Like shouting or yelling?"

"Who shouted?"

"Everyone. Mom and Dad and sometimes even Carolyn or Maria."

"What were the arguments about?"

"About Daddy Ray, I mean my father, not working when he would go to be drunk every day. And a lot about the keys to cars or trucks. He would swear and end up walking up to Beano's, the bar at the top of the hill. Sometimes Mom bought him his own bottle of Four Roses, which was whiskey that didn't smell like roses."

"How did you feel when they argued?"

"Unhappy, maybe."

"Scared?"

"Not really. They were just loud. It was just loud talking."

"Did anyone ever hit?"

"Just once that I ever saw. Bonnie Mom hit Dad with a slap across his face."

"What can you tell me about that?"

"It was one time when Mom had hid all the keys to the trucks and car and Dad was mad about that and then Mom slammed a bottle of Four Roses on the kitchen table and she said if you want to drink, then drink, and then she said that she'd drink too, that they could both get drunk and not work. She got two glasses and poured some for each of them and Daddy Ray said a funny toast but of course Mom didn't laugh. But then they sat silent, sort of staring for a long time. I was sitting on the open side of the stairs and the silence and staring went on and on. And then, just like from nothing, Mom slapped Daddy Ray across the face really hard and she started to cry and ran upstairs past me. Daddy Ray just sat there drinking his drink and he drank Mom's drink too."

"How did you feel?"

"I forget. I mean I never knew how I felt."

Dr. Brenaman wrote some things on his paper.

Because I didn't know why I was in psychiatric, I didn't know how telling about my feelings would help me get out. In tutoring I learned that the questions were the most important part of learning. John said it was questions that made new ways of thinking.

I liked my little room, but I couldn't go there without permission. Homework time was at the tables in the game room for our group, the same kids that were together with Dr. Miller in group therapy. Jack's group went to the library for homework.

With tutoring and homework and therapies, there was hardly any time to think about feelings much. By the time I was alone in my room; it was sleepy feelings and then sleep. I missed Bonnie Mom and Daddy Ray and my sisters. I wanted to go home. But mostly I wanted to be out and alone. Maybe I wouldn't even be here if I hadn't ran into Cappy that day, if I didn't help him read his *Field and Stream* and if I hadn't wanted to show him the rifle and if I hadn't ran. If was an always favorite word because of how it held things in their maybe. But now I saw how the ifs can back up, if and if and if.

---

if

/if/

conjunction

on the condition or supposition that; in the event that.

My best alone time, was inside my books. The library at psychiatric meant I had hundreds of books. I just found out that this was just the kid's library. So that was why all the books were so right. I checked out a book by Jack London. One day in the game room I showed it to Jack, covering up the name London with my hand.

"I see you wrote a book, Jack," I said.

"Yep. Something to do while biding my time in the looney bin."

"What's biding my time mean?"

"You know, it's like treading water. You don't drown but you don't get anywhere either." The swimming instructor, Sally, had taught the starters group how to tread water, so I knew what that meant. "But you never bide your time, do you Brainy? You always got somewhere to get to, that's for sure. So, what did I name that book?" Jack asked.

"*The Call of the Wild*," I said. Jack did a great imitation of a howling wolf or coyote, or dog. I looked at him direct in a stare and did a quiet long growl. He stared back and gave out a bunch of barks. I barked back and he answered it with another bark. We went back and forth with barks and growls.

"Knock it off guys," Alvin, the orderly supervising us, said. Someone was almost always supervising us which was just a bigger word for watching us. Jack shrugged.

"Catch you later, Brainy."

When I started reading *Call of the Wild*, I had to use my dictionary four times in the first four lines. Nomadic meant wandering. Chafing was like when you rubbed against a shovel handle and sort of blistered.

Brumal was winter things. Ferine meant feral. I had to look up feral too and it became my new favorite word and one of the words that hung in the air like a sign. In tutoring, John always talked about ideas and how so many things were someone's idea and how someone maybe gave that idea a word. Feral made me think of the smell of the earth when I'm on my back looking at the sky. Feral and the ideas it connected to, seeped into the water well of me, down and deep and true. Like when Jack and I were playing at wolf dogs. I felt the growl of it. Feral was an idea far from words, and yet it was a word, taming that idea for anyone who named it.

---

feral
/ˈferəl, ˈfirəl/

adjective
especially of an animal, in a wild state, especially after escape from captivity or domestication.

I thought the book might really be slow reading, but by the second chapter I had fallen in love with Buck, and the sentences seemed to tell me what the words meant. Buck was a huge dog whose father was a Saint Bernard and whose mother was a Scotch Shepherd. It was Buck's story. It made me think about how things happen. It made me feel you just have to find a way to live in your own story. I wanted to explain that to Dr. Brenaman, because it was a feeling. But I never got a chance, even though I saw him almost every day. He would say good morning or good afternoon when he came to get me, but then he'd never speak until we got back to his office and he sat behind his desk.

"Did you spend time with your father in the slaughterhouse?"

"I had to go to school."

"When you weren't in school."

Dr. Brenaman's questions needed long answers. He didn't like when you just said yes or just said no. "I'd sometimes pull the hoist to lift the cow or hold the hose to wash the blood down the drain. I sometimes cranked the machine that made the sausage, but then they got an electric one and you didn't need to crank it."

"What other ways did you help?"

"I liked to rub the curing salt into the bacon before it got smoked. In the shop I could rake the sawdust that kept the floor from getting greasy and sometimes sweep it up and put down new sawdust. I wasn't allowed to touch the slicer or knives."

"Did your sisters help out too?"

"No. They did girl things in the house. The shop and slaughterhouse was boy things."

"But your mother worked in the shop."

"That was different, she was the boss. Especially if my father was, well, not there."

"Why wouldn't he be there?"

"You already know that, don't you? He was drinking whiskey until he couldn't anymore."

"How long would that be?"

"A long time. Not like Mickey Rooney in the movie, just the one day. Lots of days, weeks."

"Months?"

"No. Two or three weeks, maybe."

"Did you like to help in the slaughterhouse?"

"No."

"Why?"

"I didn't like to see the animals killed. The other jobs were okay. I was allowed to go play most of the time. I didn't have to help if I didn't want to, not like I had to go to school." I wanted to say, not like I have to be in psychiatric and answer all these questions and have my answers written down. But I didn't.

"Who did you play with?"

"By myself."

"Did you like that?"

"Yes. It's the best." Then I just blurted it out. "I wish I could be alone. I wish I could go home. When will I go home?"

"I don't think you're ready, Billy."

"Okay," I said. And then the talk doc session was over. I heard Cappy's voice in my head, "Hell, I'm ready. I'm goddamned ready to go home." But all I said was okay.

I always walked behind Dr. Brenaman from wherever he picked me up, to his office. He walked slowly because of his limp and the way his one leg that had a brace and a different shoe dragged behind. I never asked him about that. It didn't seem polite and he was the one who mainly asked questions. Except the day he explained about the special doctor.

"Next week you will be seeing another doctor for a consultation."

"What's a consultation?"

"Well, she's a specialist, here from Philadelphia, Dr. Logan. I want her to talk with you. In fact she's coming just to talk with you."

"Why is she special?"

"She only works with youngsters your age."

"Oh. When?"

"For four days next week, starting Tuesday. It will take most of each day."

"I have tutor."

"We'll reschedule that."

"Does John know?"

"Yes, it's already been arranged. You won't miss anything. I understand you're doing really well with your lessons. What book are you reading now?"

"*The Call of the Wild*."

"What's it about?"

"A dog."

"Good. That's all for today, Billy."

When I left Dr. Brenaman, I knew a feeling. I knew a name for it. It was like I was being arranged.

arrange

/əˈrānj/

verb

put things in a neat, attractive, or required order.

●

When his patient had left, Allen Brenaman pulled the file labeled William Calvin and placed the hand written notes on top of the typed notes from previous sessions. He had another appointment in an hour, in his first floor outpatient office. William Calvin was the only patient he had that was institutionalized, a word that he hated. Like he always did after a session, he turned out the lights and sat back at his desk in the darkened office. The only window looked out on the enclosed courtyard. He liked the way the sliver of light cut across the room. He needed to compose a memo as a follow-up to the phone conversation he had earlier with Captain O'Hara, the police officer, who still handled the legal component to William Calvin's case. He typed directly into his new Remington, one of the perks of the job. Western in general and the experimental children's ward in particular were very well funded. He typed:

> Western Psychiatric could not consider your suggested six month institutional stay as a guideline in any decision concerning discharge.

He removed the paper crumpled it into a ball and started over; just to change the word could to would. In the phone conversation he had said, "We're not a prison," but he stopped short of including that in his written memo.

While all of his patients were minors, he had never had one as young as William Calvin. It was his idea to bring in Helen Logan. They were close friends and had been more than that for a short time during medical school at Johns Hopkins. Still, he was uneasy about how quickly she had jumped at the offer. She was practically creating the standard protocols in pediatric psychiatry for her specialty in early childhood development and aberration. She had not only requested his complete file and notes but all records from Connie Bencloski, the director of psychiatric social services. She even had obtained the legal files from the police precinct that had handled the incident leading to William Calvin's admission to Western Psychiatric.

His paper on repression in children had been well received, both in its presentation at the conference and after its publication in the *American Journal of Psychiatry*. But lately, something seemed to be slipping out of his grasp. He always felt that his training in medical school, with its rigor of assessing and acting, collided with the training in his psychiatric specialty that required nudging, silence, and waiting. He finished typing,

> We are a short term facility with an average stay of three months and a maximum stay of eight months. Our protocol of intensive varied therapies has had a very high success rate with the lowest recidivism ever recorded. William Calvin will be evaluated within our guidelines.

He pushed his typewriter back and rested his head on the desk.

○

I was glad I hadn't missed physical therapy which was dodgeball. I felt different. I was teasing the other team with loud calls, bragging that no one could get me out. Jack was on the opposite team and I had him laughing so hard that I easily hit him with my usual slow pitch. I talked more than I ever did at dinner. Jack stopped by our table and said "Don't worry, his talk doc forgot to flip his off switch."

That night I had a hard time getting to sleep. I awoke in the middle of the night, startled by someone standing over me. It was Jack. He was shaking and breathing funny. "Hey, Brainy," he said. "Can I lay here for a bit? I'm . . ."

When he didn't finish I said sure and he crawled in beside me facing the far wall. That was when his funny breathing turned into sobs and more shaking. I rubbed his back for a while and then put my arm around him and he breathed more softly. I whispered a poem I had learned last week about how two paths went in different directions, and then Jack was asleep. I woke up and it was still dark but starting to break light on the far hill. I woke Jack up because we were breaking a big rule with him sleeping there. He snuck across to the bathroom and was able to walk back to the dormitory like he was peeing in the middle of the night and he never did get caught.

●

Tom, the orderly who had the night shift, saw on one of his rounds that Jack was not in his bed in the dormitory. When he checked Billy's room he saw Jack lying in Billy's bed, his body heaving in uncontrollable sobs, silent except for a tiny gasp to gain his breath. He saw Billy rubbing his back gently and heard the beginning of Billy whispering the Robert Frost poem. He should have recorded it, reported it. He should have penalized both boys. But, he didn't. Tom had worked at Western Psychiatric for nine years now and he saw again and again the ways of change that put these stranded children back into a world they could manage. And well you couldn't tell, you just never knew.

CHAPTER 20

The Special Doctor

LIKE JAMES, as soon as I wanted to go home, it scared me to want it. Or scared me to maybe get what I wanted. I loved the learning with John. I started thinking of him as Mr. Gibbon because I wanted him to be an always regular teacher.

In so many ways, I liked psychiatric. I had friends and books and art and games that made me forget how arranged I felt, how locked the doors were.

---

either

/ˈēTHər, ˈīTHər/

conjunction & adverb
used before the first of two or more alternatives that are being specified, the other being introduced by or.

I felt something stuck about the questions I never asked Jack about that time he came to my room. I kept repeating in my head the Jack Frost poem I had said aloud that night to calm him. No, ha, ha. Jack is the one who paints the windows icy. Robert wrote the poem. Anyhow, I kept thinking about the roads you could or couldn't travel, I kept thinking about the because reason, the cause of the effect like I learned when I was little. Of course I knew you could not travel both. I saw *either* and *or* as little signs beside *in* and *out*. Like the signs that named all the streets in Pittsburgh. Turn left. Turn right. But maybe this is a one way, and not the way you can travel. And then there's the both that you can never travel. That both settled into me in a growl, feral and restless. I should have asked Jack about something.

----

or

/ôr/

conjunction
used to link alternatives.

Doctor Logan was special, but I still wasn't sure why. I thought she'd be old like Mrs. Bencloski, the first lady who talked to me when I came here. Mrs. Bencloski looked like Dick and Jane's grandmother in my old reading book. I didn't have any grandmas or grandpas because Bonnie Mom was an orphan and Daddy Ray ran away and never looked back. I heard him say that in just that way more than once. So there were no grandmas. I guess they disappear if you never look back.

But Dr. Logan was young and pretty, like Joanne and Bonnie Mom and she smiled a lot and even laughed sometimes.

She gave me her own tests the whole first day and I had to say answers out loud without thinking. Of course that's impossible, so I just thought real fast. It seemed maybe she wasn't a talk doc, but then she was.

"So, Billy, do you know why you're here?"

"Because the doors are locked," I said. Actually that was Darryl's joke first and when I told Dr. Brenaman, he didn't smile. But Dr. Logan really laughed.

"Tell me about the day you took your father's rifle."

"Well, let me see. It was a good day to show Cappy that he was wrong about the rifle, just like he was about the rotten egg water."

"Whoa, whoa, whoa," Dr. Logan said, smiling big. I liked that, because it was horse talk like Mickey Rooney used. It meant slow down, wait a minute. "Who is Cappy, and what's rotten egg water?" she said.

"Well, Cappy's my friend if I ran into him at the playground. He was just starting first grade and I helped him not be so worried about that. He thought everyone in town had rotten egg water which tastes funny and when I said we didn't, he didn't believe me. My Mom told me the funny taste was from sulfur that the coal mines made go into the water. Our well was on a steep hill away from the mines."

"And what does this have to do with the rifle?"

I laughed. "I used to never like to talk, and now I talk too much," I said. "The because answer is, one day when I had a bottle of our water at the playground, I gave it to Cappy to drink and then he believed me."

"First of all, don't worry about talking too much. We have all the time we need. I want you to explain it to me. Why was it a good day to show Cappy he was wrong about the rifle?"

"Because the slaughterhouse was closed for the day so Daddy Ray could go to an early AA meeting. He wouldn't need the rifle, so I could show Cappy he was wrong and then put it back."

"How was Cappy wrong?"

I liked that Dr. Logan asked how, and not why. It was a different question and it made me talk different. "Do you want to know all the talk, like when it started?"

"Yes."

"Well, Cappy can't read and he liked that I could read and memorize. One day he needed some reading in an old magazine so I read him about Jimmy's first gun, in the *Field and Stream*. It was a Remington."

"So this was an advertisement?"

You had to know that Dr. Logan's sentences were really questions by listening to her voice. "Yes," I said. Did you know they didn't make Remington rifles during the war because they needed to make guns to fight?"

"No, I didn't know that. But why would you decide to take your father's rifle to the playground when you weren't even allowed to touch the knives or slicers?"

"How did you know that?"

"I read Doctor Brenaman's notes."

"He likes to write things down."

"Do you not like that?"

"No, it's like I'm a puzzle and he's arranging the pieces."

"Well, he wants to help you. I'll write notes too, but not while we're talking. So you read the advertisement to Cappy."

"Why do I need help?

"I don't know Billy. I really don't. Listen, it's against the law to shoot at anyone. Officer Kane said you shot the rifle when you were near third base."

"You know Officer Kane?"

"I spoke with him on the phone, and with Captain O'Hara."

"Why."

"So I could understand what happened the day you took your father's rifle."

"Why?"

"So I could help Doctor Brenaman help you."

"Oh. Why do I need help?"

"Do you know what happened that day?"

"It's mixed up I guess."

"Let's stop for today. I don't want you to be late for dinner. You'll have lessons tomorrow morning with Mr. Gibbon, then you'll meet me in Doctor Brenaman's office after lunch at one o'clock. I've written it down for you."

Dr. Logan came around the desk and handed me a card. Then she stooped down and gave me a hug. "You seem pretty happy, Billy. Are you happy?"

"Is happy a feeling?"

"Yes. A good feeling, like when you wake up and are glad to be awake."

"Yes, I'm happy."

"Good. I'll see you tomorrow."

Helen Logan crossed back to the desk to record her notes. She wrote: "Is happy a feeling?" For her, the advantage of making notes after a session was that the recall acted as an automatic ordering of what was important. She didn't like the way the session had gotten off track. She took off the jacket of her dress and piled her hair up, pinning it carelessly. When Allen Brenaman had asked her to consult on this case she already had a newspaper article of the incident leading to William Calvin's admission. It was in a file labeled aberrant behavior in early childhood. She read several times Allen's paper on repression and its references to the Calvin case. She had read all of his notes and the notes from the precinct officers. She wrote, "The patient feels like he's being made into a puzzle and the pieces need to be arranged." This was bothersome because it was a puzzle and nothing seemed to fit and she hated seeing it that way.

She picked up the phone and dialed the office of psychiatric social services. When she was finally connected to the director, she wasn't sure why she had called. "Connie, hi, it's Helen Logan. How are you?"

"I'm well, thank you. I heard you were in town."

"I'm doing a consultation for Allen Brenaman on the William Calvin case. Can I set up a time to talk to you?"

"Sure, what's your schedule?"

"Anytime in the morning."

"I have an eight o'clock appointment, but I could see you, say nine thirty."

"Thanks Connie, I appreciate it. I'll see you then." Helen only knew Connie Bencloski professionally, but she had known her for years. The hospital that Helen Logan was affiliated with, Eastern Psychiatric, often met with staff from Western Psychiatric. The two were connected in some way that Helen wasn't sure of, funding, board of directors, mission statements, the kind of thing that she generally ignored. She felt anxious to be going into this meeting not sure of why she had even scheduled it.

Especially with Connie Bencloski who had literally been in psychiatric social work since before Helen was born.

More than that she had begun to feel that Allen Brenaman was wrong about William Calvin and she didn't relish the idea of telling him that. Allen was highly esteemed, practically famous. It didn't help that he was an old friend. In fact it made it worse. "Is happiness a feeling?" she said out loud.

○

I was excited about tutoring. We had tutoring even though it was Friday, to make up the time we missed for me to go to Doctor Logan. In yesterday's shorter lesson James and I had put white carnations in red, blue and green water we had made with drops of food coloring. Mr. Gibbon said we'd see tomorrow what happens because it was a science experiment and we would observe the results which meant take a look.

When I got to the library, I couldn't believe it. James was really surprised too. Mr. Gibbon gave us a big word for the lesson, transpiration. That was the word for how the molecules climbed up the stem against gravity and changed the white flowers to red or blue or green. Molecule was a word we had learned before. I loved that word and the word we had learned with it, atom. I loved the tiny, tiny world they told about. It made me think of the teeny-tiny woman in the teeny-tiny house from a story when I was little. But molecules and atoms were even smaller than that, invisible and sort of magical.

"Can I do the experiment over and take a flower with me so I can watch?" I said.

"Sure. I have to check with Nurse Higgins, but I think it would be okay. It's in a plastic tube. I have more flowers in the refrigerator downstairs. I'll get one for you and one for James if you're allowed."

When we got permitted, we each filled another plastic test tube with water. I made mine blue and James made his red. James put his on the stand by his bed in the dormitory. But I carried mine with me everywhere. At lunch I watched the white flower the whole time I ate.

I was always good at waiting. I was learning to be good at watching too, watching so closely I might spot a change even if it was very, very slowly pushing against gravity, which seemed impossible.

●

By the time Helen Logan was seated in Mrs. Bencloski's waiting room, she had made a page of notes clarifying her questions. She looked fresh, alert, but she felt a kind of exhaustion. It was the kind that had less to do with rest and more to do with the drain you felt when you couldn't remember something that you knew. Like taking a test in which none of the answers or all of the answers seemed right. She dumped a puzzle with oversize pieces on the table but she couldn't focus enough to put it together.

"The little boy's holding the plane," Connie Bencloski said.

"Connie, it's great to see you. Thanks for making time. I know how busy you are."

"I won't deny it. Let's go in my office. So what can I help you with? This is the William Calvin case. We sent you my notes."

"Yes. Thanks for that. I've met with him twice. Long sessions. I'll see him later today, tomorrow for a shorter time because of visitors in the afternoon, and that's it." The realization of that timetable suddenly struck her as absurd and she lost her train of thought.

"What can I clarify for you?"

Helen glanced at her notes. "What factors figured into his being institutionalized? He's very young even for the children's ward."

"Yes, certainly. His age was a concern. But the legal pressure, the kind of community fear an incident like this creates were all part of the consideration."

"Your notes seemed to center around the idea of revenge. What gave you that impression?"

"You know, I wasn't completely convinced about the motive of revenge. There was nothing vengeful or even angry that I saw initially."

"I'm not seeing the repressed anger that Dr. Brenaman describes."

"I see. Well." Connie took a minute to regain her train of thought. "What I noted was strong recall detail, very strong concerning not being allowed to play ball with the other kids. Also from other children, interviewed for the police report, some incident in which he was promised he could play if he didn't strike out, but then they broke their promise and said he couldn't play. He corroborated this and made a special point that he didn't cry."

"I understand that since being here he has never exhibited any crying or anger or even disgruntlement."

"I've seen those reports. That's key to Allen's conclusions of repression."

"He says he's happy."

"Only modern psychiatry could make happiness a symptom."

Helen laughed. "Do you know of a boy in the town named Cappy McLaughlin? He would have been there that day of the shooting. But not one of the boys playing ball."

"Not off hand. Let me check the file. He must be Harrold McLaughlin, age six. He has twin sisters, age thirteen. Only Darlene was at the playground when the incident occurred. They were seated on an embankment with two other girls. The other ten children listed were on the ball field."

"Yesterday, I saw John Gibbon's standardized test results. Can that be accurate? Billy's reading at a ninth grade level."

"I heard him read. That doesn't surprise me."

"Last question. What does the six month recommendation for institutionalizing mean? Who determines that?" She realized she sounded accusatory and wasn't surprised that Connie responded defensively.

"It's just a guideline. This isn't punitive. It's valuable for the child to be out of the community, to allow the incident to recede, fade. No one was hurt. It's really an idea that needs to fade."

Helen found herself making her first note. She wrote, "It's really an idea that needs to fade."

○

My carnation was still completely white when lunch was over. I explained to Darryl that something was happening even though you can't see it yet because the atoms and molecules are so tiny they're invisible. Somebody said that's why they call me Brainy. After lunch I took it with me to see Doctor Logan.

"What do you have there?"

"An experiment."

"That's very interesting."

"The white flower will turn blue. We did it once, but I wanted to see it. It's called transportation."

"Transpiration."

"Yes, that's it. You know about that?"

"Oh yes. It's very fascinating, but it's slow. I'm not sure you can see it."

"Okay. But I want to try."

"I want to pick up where we left off yesterday. I want you to not be mixed up about that day you took your father's rifle. When you read the advertisement to Cappy about the young boy's first gun, what did you tell him that he didn't believe?"

"That I had a rifle like that. I explained it wasn't really mine but that I got to hold it sometimes."

"Was that true?"

"No. Only once."

"And what did Cappy say when you told him that?

"Well, Cappy swears a lot and he's a funny talker but he didn't believe me."

"So you thought you'd take the rifle and show him?"

This was a question and I said, "Yes."

"How long after that day did you take the rifle?"

"I don't know, another week or so."

"The reason I said Dr. Brenaman wanted to help you and I want to help you is that well, what you did was against the law. It was dangerous. Someone could have been hurt or even killed. You could have killed someone."

"Killed? Like Daddy Ray kills the cows? Like killing in a war?"

"Yes. Were you angry at those boys?"

"No."

"You knew the gun could kill. You watched your father kill the cows with it."

"Yes."

"Did you think, I'll show them? They'll be sorry?"

"No. Boys have to kill when the war comes. I'm not a baby. I'm not a crybaby. But I don't want to grow up and kill like in my bad dream. Lena doesn't have to. Eleanor doesn't have to. It's just that I ran. I shouldn't have ran. I saw Cappy on the bank and I ran. I wanted to show Cappy that I wasn't a liar and I wouldn't burn in hell though maybe that was just a joke. I just wanted to show Cappy."

"So now we both understand that day a bit better. Don't we, Billy?"

"Yes."

"I have a few more tests I'd like to give you. Is that okay?"

"As long as there's no spelling."

"No spelling. I promise."

"Look," I said. "There's tiny, tiny edges of blue on each petal."

"Wow!" Dr. Logan said.

"I know," I said. "Wow."

CHAPTER 21

Change

WHEN I WOKE UP the next morning, my flower was completely blue. Even though I knew it would happen, I was so excited to see it. It made me think that what I told Doctor Logan was the true thing. I was happy.

That visitor's day was the best. It was Mom and Daddy Ray and Maria. And guess what? Eleanor and Lena got to come for a special visit. At first they seemed very quiet and different but then they had lots of things to tell me. Mom announced that we were all going out to lunch at a restaurant that had a table for us no matter how crowded they were because we had a reservation, which meant they knew we were coming.

---

reservation

/ˌrezərˈvāSH(ə)n/

noun
an arrangement whereby something, especially a seat or room, is booked for a particular person.

Daddy Ray said that since they knew we were coming they had baked a cake, which was a funny song he used to sing. And they did too, with chocolate icing and a scoop of ice cream.

It's funny but the best special time makes you sad when it's over because you're in and they are out and going back home which was the maybe reason visitor's day had so many kids upset.

Also, that evening, a new kid came on our floor who wouldn't stop screaming. He had to go in a special room, different than the room you were put in if you were fighting or in other trouble. You could hear his screams everywhere. Alvin, the orderly, said that the shot they gave him could have put a horse to sleep. By the time the boy quieted down, and with visitor's day and everything, the something in the air was really something.

On top of all that, it was also the day I said goodbye to Dr. Logan who was going back to Philadelphia. I thanked her and said I was glad to meet her. I didn't say I wished she was my everyday talk doc, but I sort of did. But, I did like Doctor Brenaman, even if he didn't smile.

●

Allen Brenaman thought it was a mistake to not confer with Helen Logan until after her four sessions with William Calvin. They had dinner together the evening she arrived, but he hadn't seen her since. That schedule had been her idea, and at the time it didn't seem right, but she was sort of doing him a favor. What he wanted from that favor seemed more muddled than ever.

Damned if he knew why her being ten minutes late made him feel at a disadvantage; why did he even see this consultation as adversarial, with advantages and disadvantages?

Helen Logan gave a single knock and pushed the office door open at the same time.

"Sorry I'm late. I realized I was better off packing and going directly to the train station from here." She set a suitcase in the corner. "Nice office. Pretty different from that black box you had me working in."

"I'm usually there most days too. I did vote for the smaller private in-patient offices over the larger shared ones, so I can't complain."

"I can't either," Helen said. She sat directly across from him. Her familiar scent, Chanel Number Five, added to his unease.

"So, William Calvin is no longer a statistic on a page. How did it go?"

"He's very charming."

"I was afraid he might charm you."

"What does that mean?"

"Just that the compliant sweet ones often get overlooked, unlike the problem cases."

"Happiness as a symptom," Helen said.

"He shot a .22 rifle into a group of boys playing ball who had a history of excluding him."

"I focused all of my sessions, outside of testing, on that incident and the weeks leading up to it."

"And?"

"I find it difficult to assign intention."

"Intention is difficult to discern when there's repression."

"Allen, I'm not seeing repression. I'll need a few weeks to get you my report, but I'm just not seeing it."

"It's a classic case. You just can't look at that charming little boy in isolation. The father kills animals for a livelihood. The house is on the same property as the slaughterhouse."

Helen had begun shaking her head slowly in the middle of Allen's sentence. A habit he had always found annoying. "I see a remarkable level of individuation for a six year old," she said.

"Look Helen, I think some of these Jungian constructs have value. But you can't mix these ideas without muddling the whole diagnosis. The father is a binge alcoholic vacillating between playful and loving and irresponsible and abusive. What you're seeing as happiness is just a vulnerable child in a safe place."

"I see your point Allen, I really do. But from the perspective of early childhood development, William Calvin exhibits remarkable progress toward normal maturation. He reads at a ninth grade level."

"He's an extreme loner, living in a world of fiction."

"Not according to the nurses notations. I see words like affable, social, and friendly."

"In a protected environment. But he longs for the opportunity to be alone."

"I know the feeling."

Allen finally smiled. "Me, too. Thanks for the input Helen. I'm not dismissing it."

"He took the gun to the playground to show his friend Cappy. I think the firing of the gun was an accident."

Allen started to make a note but decided against it. "The incident was a big deal in that small town. He needs to be away from that environment, not to mention the home environment. He needs our help."

"He asked me, Why do I need help?"

"Remember, some of what you're seeing is progress. He's been here almost four months."

"Eight months is the maximum stay here," Helen said. "Please tell me you won't recommend further in-patient therapy elsewhere."

"You mean a state facility? Never. You need to catch a train."

"I know. I'm glad I met him. It's given me a lot to think about."

"It was good seeing you," Allen said. They both stood. The hug was awkward. It was all confusing.

○

I woke up the next morning thinking about the screaming new boy even though there was silence. The chimes sounded seven times. It was seven o'clock. When we gathered at the nurse's station for breakfast, I saw the new boy standing away from the group. "Good morning," I said. "My name's Billy." I touched his arm and he flinched back. "What's your name?" He didn't answer. Tom came over and said, "This is David." When we got to the cafeteria, I explained to David how to get a tray for his food and stuff. He did what I told him, but he never spoke. I was used to being friendly with Arnie who never said anything. I told him to sit with us at our table. I told everyone his name was David and they just sort of nodded. Even James, who tried to smile, eyed David cautiously.

Silence is a funny thing. I loved words. But I loved silence too. I watched David's silence all through breakfast. I wished I could give him a word to help his screaming self.

Everything changes. When we had the monthly checkup the nurse said I grew another inch and gained three pounds. We went swimming once more. I was getting really good. We had a movie on Halloween that was moving drawings. I liked the real people movie better, but this was fun too. We each got a small plastic pumpkin with a miniature pinball game in it and an apple, but no candy. Darryl said that was because candy would make us all crazy and Paul said, don't you mean crazier. I never used words like crazy or nut or looney because they weren't nice and I didn't really know what they meant.

I didn't wake up that morning until I heard the general morning bell that meant we had to be out of bed. I gathered my dirty clothes together in my net bag and put it outside my door. There were lots of routines in psychiatric that I just did without thinking. I guess that's why they called them routine.

Some changes aren't so good. News is about change. Not on the radio news but like when James said, "I got some news." The good news and the bad news was the same news. James was going home. Discharged. He was glad and that was the good part. The bad part was inside of me.

I hugged him. "When?" I said.

"Next Tuesday. Not tomorrow, a week from tomorrow. I'm glad. I'm really ready this time. I'm not depressed anymore." James and I were in the small lounge at the end of the hall, closer to the nurse's station. In group therapy, with Dr. Miller, James talked about depressed sometimes, but I didn't really understand.

"What is depressed, exactly?" I asked.

"I can't explain it. My doctor told me that's what I was when I came here. It's dark and empty. I know when it goes away."

"Dark and empty," I said. "I'm glad depressed is gone and you're going home, but I'm really, really going to miss you."

"Thanks, Brainy. I'll miss you too. You know, you really helped me, especially in tutoring. You helped me remember how fun it was to learn."

"John makes it really fun."

"Yes. I'll miss him too but I know I'm ready to go home."

"Why did they bring you here?"

"Because I tried to kill myself."

"Kill yourself?" I said. "Like in a war? A war against yourself?"

"Sort of."

"Oh, James." I hugged him again. He cried and smiled at the same time like when the sun comes out but it's still raining.

"And the war's over?" I said it like a question.

"Yep," James said.

"And you can go home because it's over, over there."

"What do you mean?"

"Like in the world war song that says, 'We won't go home 'til it's over, over there.'"

James laughed. "Yeah, I remember that song. He showed me his wrists. "I cut myself. I almost bled to death."

I touched his scars. I had never even seen them and they were right there. "Like Arnie, trying to bleed out the dark and empty," I said.

"I think I wanted to disappear," James said. "But then I was glad I was here and now I'll be glad to be home."

"Like when you wake up, and you're glad to be awake."

"Yes."

"You know what, James? You're happy."

"Yes."

When next Tuesday came, I saw James at breakfast and then I didn't see him anywhere because he was out and I was in. I tried to make the bad part about James going home that was stuck inside me change to good but I couldn't. It faded like when the movie picture slowly changes by getting dimmer and dimmer. Most things are like that, just fading.

CHAPTER 22

Wide

WITH JAMES it took a long time for the missing to fade, and it still lives like an always flicker inside me. It's not like the missing of my sisters and Bonnie Mom and Daddy Ray because I knew I'd never see James again. Here's the surprise thing. There's a part of James that he left with me and it's in me too. It's a connection to some feeling when I hugged him and something I began to know about sadness. James' sadness but my feeling. I wanted to name it, but I can't. When I think of it I name it "wide." It's just a nickname like Brainy for me and Pitt for Pittsburgh. But someday I'll learn a word big enough to be its real name.

Since asking James why he came here, I felt more and more that I needed to ask Jack why he came. But I could touch James' scars because they were the remains of a thing that's healed. I looked, but Jack never showed a scar. Because he was too old to be in my group therapy, I didn't even have the clues that got said when Dr. Miller asked, "What's happening in the group?" What if there was no scar because nothing was healed? Like how Arnie banged his head so he wouldn't lose the hurt into a yesterday because he needed to remember it.

Jack was in the special room for having smashed his cup in occupational therapy. He had made it with the clay and it came out of the oven and it was really nice, but he just threw it really hard and smashed it into pieces and although it didn't hit anyone, he's still in the special room. Maybe it's like how I'm still in psychiatric even though the bullet that shot from Daddy Ray's .22 rifle hit the dirt and stuck in the bottom of the pole for the backstop. I just learned that from Doctor Brenaman. He's starting to tell me things instead of just asking questions about stuff he already knows.

David, the screaming boy who went silent, started talking. He just talked regular. He was nice, I liked him. Mr. Gibbon and I met for two weeks with just me and then one day he told me David would be joining us. David was in sixth grade so we wouldn't be having any of the lessons together like James and I did.

Instead of just thinking it, I started calling John, Mr. Gibbon. He never mentioned the change. My biggest worry about getting out of psychiatric was school. Although Joanne had told me the last time she visited, that I wouldn't go back to my old school. Instead I would go to Saint Edward's School which was part of our church that we never went to.

Mr. Gibbon said I could skip the rest of second grade and the first half of third grade, that I already had those skills.

---

skill

/skil/

noun

the ability to do something well; expertise.

Mr. Gibbon liked to talk about skills. Skills weren't the learning really. It was like getting good at using the potter's wheel wasn't the bowl, but it could get you a bowl. Mr. Gibbon had a way of laughing at my good scores, that I liked.

"Hey, Billy. Look what I just got in." He would be laughing so he almost couldn't say it. "Ninety-six percentile. That's almost fifth grade. And in math, the subject you claim you're not good at." Pennsylvania said I had to pass certain level tests while I was in tutoring. That's how Mr. Gibbon knew I could go to the second half of third grade. Jack said his tests were from Delaware and that he was a little bit behind but a lot further ahead than he was at his old school.

A few days after Jack got out of the special room he had a fight and even hit the orderly who tried to break it up. This time he was in for three whole days, for meals and therapies and everything. He could be heard yelling from the special room. When he came out, he was silent and sullen and his stare was glassy eyed and didn't meet your eyes even when he said something to you. Which he almost never did.

Jack's meanness and fighting was never at me. I figured Jack was like Buck, the dog in *Call of the Wild*. He wanted to find an old way of breathing, the way outside of the anger, because he was so good. Buck wanted to live in the places that weren't wild, but in the end he knew he couldn't. But there was no good wild to live in for people. People have to stop when the sign says stop, and go the one way that the arrow points and learn the little names of the streets so we can return to where we want to be.

Because Jack didn't talk much lately, I'd just give him a hug from behind when he was sitting and he'd say, "Hi, Brainy."

"Swimming's coming up tomorrow," I said. I knew that for Jack, the water was one place he could find his old way of breathing. He was like a champion swimmer. The instructor for the advanced kids said he could probably train for the Olympics, the world contests that happened again in two more summers. Of course Jack wouldn't be old enough then but maybe someday.

"They took swimming away 'cause I fight too much," Jack said.

"Whoa, whoa, whoa," I said. Like Doctor Logan's horse talk for hold up. "They can't do that."

"They can. They did. I deserve it."

Deserve was an odd word. It meant you earned it, because of what you did, but what you earned could be good or bad.

deserve

/dəˈzərv/

verb

do something or have or show qualities worthy of reward or punishment.

"I'll be back," I said.

I went to the nurse's station. Luckily, both Nurse Higgins and Tom, my favorite orderly were there. I was always behaved. I mean well behaved. Mr. Gibbon said I have to watch my grammar which is sort of like making your bed with everything neat although it's still a bed. But grammar stuff can sometimes get in the way. What I want to explain is that because I was always well behaved, because I always listened, I deserved to be listened to.

"Miss Higgins, I need a very big favor," I said. She and Tom both laughed.

"If I can," she said.

"Jack has to go swimming tomorrow. He has to."

"Jack has no privileges for another week. He knows that. Did he ask you to come to me?"

"No. Jack doesn't know I'm asking. But he needs to swim. The swimmer is the best Jack. It's who he really is."

"You're right, Brainy," Tom said. That's kind of a funny way of putting it, but it is who Jack really is."

Nurse Higgins grabbed her notepad and began to write. Not just a note, but a whole bunch of words. I just stood there watching her and she wrote and wrote. Finally she looked up.

"I'll tell Jack he can go swimming," she said.

I was very surprised to see her no turn into yes. "Thanks," I said. "He's in the game room."

"Tom," Nurse Higgins said. "Will you go tell Jack that he can go swimming?"

Tom grabbed my head and gave me a knuckle rub. When I saw Jack later he said, "I know you did it for me, thanks." I shrugged the way Jack always did. A shrug was a useful thing. It said so much. I liked the way it whispered, a quiet sure or unsure.

After swimming, Jack started talking regular again. Much later a really, really wide thing happened. It was just after Thanksgiving. I was supposed to go home for three days at Thanksgiving. But then Daddy Ray was drinking and Doctor Brenaman said no, I could not go home. The day after Thanksgiving was quiet because the kids that were ready to try it and lived close by did go home.

Jack didn't like checkers, so he taught me how to play chess. Well, how to make the moves. I always lost. Anytime there was a holiday, there was a special visitor's day too. Joanne had come to see me from Grove City where she worked now. Jack had a visitor also. The visitors were usually in their separate rooms when we got to the fourth floor, but yesterday they were just arriving as we stepped off the elevator.

Jack took another pawn I left open. "Was the pretty girl that visited you yesterday one of your sisters?"

"Yes. That was Joanne. She's an assistant counselor person at Grove City College near here. Was that your Mom that visited you?"

"My mom's dead," Jack said.

"Oh," I said. It made me think about dead being a baby word of mine because of my sister Julie who got dead before I even got living and then the war way of making dead a part of my baby nightmares and then James' depressed that made him want to be dead or at least disappear. Anyhow it all stalled me out and I didn't know what to say.

But then Jack pushed back his chair. Clasped his hands behind his head and talked.

"I was sitting at the top of the cellar steps," he said. "My parents were in the cellar arguing. My father was swearing like he did and my mother kept saying 'I'm over', like she was some kind of a movie and it was time to role the credits. And then my father had a small gun. I missed how he went from not having it to having it. He shot my mother and she fell down slowly like she was pretending. I thought then he would see me and I remember thinking, yes, shoot me, go ahead shoot me. But then he put the gun to the side of his head and when he pulled the trigger the sound made an explosion and his head exploded out and his body kind of followed. I never shut my eyes and I never looked away. I just sat there. I was still there when the police came because the lady next door heard the shots. When the police got there, I said, 'he didn't shoot me'. I never told anyone about this, never. Everyone knew because it was big headlines but I've never told anyone until now."

I began to cry. I had never cried at psychiatric. Now I was crying in a way that I couldn't get my breath. I couldn't control it. At first Jack just shrugged. And then he started to cry too. I got up and hugged him from behind like I sometimes did and we cried and cried. When the crying finally exhausted us, I sat down and we started playing chess again. Jack beat me.

CHAPTER 23

Out

OUT WAS A ONE WAY STREET. But how to get there. Each time I heard myself say "Oh", I knew I was getting closer. "Oh" was what I said to my baby confusion, the silence that needed time to do some explaining to myself. I said "Oh" when Joanne mentioned I would go to a different school, when Mr. Gibbon said I could pick up school learning in the second half of third grade, and when Doctor Brenaman said there was a doctor I could see in Greensburg, near where I lived. Pittsburgh would be too far to drive. Oh and oh and oh.

Jack hadn't been in a fight for nearly a month and he told me he'd be going to his aunt's for three days at Christmas. I was glad to hear that because I was getting to go home for the holiday too.

There was a Christmas tree in the game room and pretend strings of holly above the nurses' station. We had a Christmas party in the cafeteria with cookies and ice cream and we got funny gifts like a plastic dinosaur or a yo-yo.

Doctor Miller played his guitar and sang mostly silly Christmas songs but my favorite Jesus carols too, with its little town of Bethlehem, and its silent night and manger with no crib. He sang good. Not like Daddy Ray who sang like a famous singer on the radio, but it was nice.

It's a funny joke now, but I thought heaven and Bethlehem were the same place. Mr. Gibbon showed me Bethlehem on the globe, and explained that heaven wasn't a place on Earth but the place some people believed you went to when you died. I liked that he said some people believed that. There was a time when James was still here that he made a lesson of explaining the difference between facts and beliefs. He loved words as much as I do. Like the skills he gave me, there were words that were tools to sort through new ideas.

He also showed me Delaware on the globe which looked really close but John said was pretty far. Distance was a strange thing, how it changed with walking or driving or flying in a plane, which I've never done. But John said the distance stayed the same, it was just the time to travel it that changed and scientists thought about that a lot.

Of all the ways of learning, I liked the thinking part the best. Although I loved to memorize and of course read. Reading was hearing another person's thinking and thinking, sometimes for years.

Two days before the Christmas visit would happen, I saw my first snowfall from way up high on the eleventh floor. It was really different to look down and follow the flakes to the ground. It made Pittsburgh as beautiful as it did my little town. It was like the wonderland song with its beautiful sight that makes you happy. It melted into dirty mush pretty fast, but it still made me happy.

When the going home time was here, Lena came with Daddy Ray to pick me up. She was really excited about Christmas. She said Santa Claus would be bringing me something special.

I said, "When out on the roof I heard such a clatter, I sprang from my bed to see what was the matter. And what to my wondering eyes should appear but a miniature sleigh and eight tiny reindeer."

Lena laughed and Daddy Ray sang the first verse of 'You Better Watch Out', the song about Santa Claus coming to town. I didn't believe that Santa Claus was a fact, but I loved the story. Still, I liked even more the idea that Daddy Ray and Mom figured out a special surprise gift for me and how much love that figuring took.

Driving home there was only a few dirty clumps of ice here and there. Everything I saw as we got closer and closer to our house said *out*. I counted each of my secret places as we drove down our road; the upper field by the stream with no houses in sight, the coke ovens abandoned and crumbling, the bridge pillars without a bridge or a road, the buttercup meadow now brown and muddy.

Crossing over Allen Creek, I could see our house as all the other houses in town disappeared. After seeing the tall beautiful buildings in Pittsburgh, it looked tiny and kind of shabby. But it was our house and the "our" part of it gave me a special tug in my stomach, which felt like I was out, even if it was only for three days.

The kitchen warmth smelled delicious. Bonnie Mom and Carolyn and Maria kept baking things to keep the delicious smells everywhere. The next day Joanne came home. We went to the Catholic church that night because Lena was an angel. I whispered to her that I knew she was really a devil, but she looked real pretty. It turned out she was one of the baby Jesus' angels that appeared to the shepherds.

When we got home, we were allowed to eat cookies and drink hot chocolate and Eleanor and Lena and I got to open one of our presents. Their presents were new nightgowns and mine was a drawing book that showed you how to draw an oak tree and a lion and lots more.

My special surprise was a two wheeler bicycle, but it did have two more wheels to train me. I rode some in the parking area. Joanne said it would be great weather for riding when I came home for good in the spring. "Oh," I said.

The day after Christmas, Bonnie Mom and Daddy Ray drove me back to psychiatric and I started to cry when I had to say goodbye. We were in the waiting room by Mrs. Bencloski's office because they were going to have a meeting, called a conference, with her. Nurse Leto came to get me and I couldn't help crying. I didn't care about being a crybaby. Since that time with Jack, I didn't think that crying was about babies at all. We needed to cry out all our sadnesses, to get in front of them, so we could see them get smaller and smaller like in Daddy Ray's rear view mirror. Mom said it wouldn't be long before I'd be home for good. Mrs. Bencloski said that was true. She probably wrote stuff down later. I said okay and went with Nurse Leto after giving more kisses.

●

Mrs. Bencloski did make a note of William Calvin's emotional response to coming back after the holiday break. Nurse Leto did as well and when Dr. Brenaman read the notes, he was encouraged.

Ray and Bonnie Calvin had scheduled the meeting to discuss the details of Billy's discharge, tentatively scheduled for April 1st of the coming year.

"The timetable exceeds the maximum stay for Western patients," Mrs. Bencloski said. But Dr. Brenaman was adamant that there was no other facility that could accommodate Billy's needs.

"And what are those?" Ray Calvin said. His tone caught Mrs. Bencloski off guard.

"Pardon me?" she said.

"What are those needs for the next three months?" He adjusted the words but not the tone.

"Well, they are a combination of Billy's personal adjustment and the situation in the community."

"This has been much longer than we had originally anticipated." Bonnie Calvin had the ability to express objections with a smile that Ray Calvin did not.

"The average stay here is three months. The maximum is eight months. We are adjusting that guideline for Billy. As you know the children's ward is fully funded. There is no charge to the families."

"I think what my husband and I are asking is, why three more months? We miss Billy. We want him home."

"That's to be expected. The community concerns have been largely abated. I'll be frank. If the home situation were more stable, it would alleviate that concern."

"We would like to sign the papers for Billy's release in the next weeks, not months." Ray Calvin stood.

"That is not an option." Mrs. Bencloski had lost her professional tone of concern.

"What? He's not up for parole yet?"

"This is not a sentence."

"Well it sure as hell sounds like it is."

"Ray, please," Bonnie said.

Ray Calvin sat back down. "None of this has been easy," he said.

"Of course not. Please continue to work with us as you have. Your cooperation has been invaluable. Both the legal and personal issues are being solved."

The meeting ended with everyone involved covering a feeling with amenable words, burying those feelings deep inside what should have been said.

---

guilt
/gilt/

noun
a feeling of deserving blame for offenses.

Ray Calvin's guilt held a shame that cradled all his love for Billy, but only surfaced as a regrettable anger.

---

blame
/blām/

verb
assign responsibility for a fault or wrong.

Bonnie Calvin had tried hard to ignore the kernel of blame that started with Ray Calvin's careless handling of the .22 rifle and grew with every drinking binge she felt obligated to report.

doubt
/dout/

noun

a feeling of uncertainty or lack of conviction.

After reading Doctor Helen Logan's report on Billy Calvin, Connie Bencloski began to doubt her decision to have institutionalized the six year old. Her whole professional esteem centered around a sense of doing good. She did not wear doubt well.

"Thank you and I'm sorry and it's to be expected and we'll be in touch and have a safe trip. Appreciate. Grateful. Understandable."

CHAPTER 24

Waiting

BEING BACK IN PSYCHIATRIC felt strange. That week when Dr. Miller asked "What's happening in the group?" everyone had something to say. A lot of the talk had to do with the holiday visit. I saw Dr. Brenaman later that day because tutoring hadn't started back up yet. We talked about me going home. The *out* sign was getting bigger and bigger and the *in* sign was getting smaller.

When I saw Jack in physical therapy he surprised me by saying he had his discharge date, January 31st. It was just a little more than a month away. Like when James was discharged, I felt glad and sad. I should have hid the sad part better.

"Hey Brainy, you'll be getting out of here pretty soon."

"Yeah, I guess. Did I tell you I'll be right in the middle of third grade when I do? It means I'm skipping. In a different school, it's a church school."

"I'll be living with my aunt in a different town," Jack said. "So I'll be going to a different school too, but I'll have to repeat the last half of fifth grade. My tutor, Mrs. Bartlett, came to my session with Dr. Ellsworth. She said its better this way. I'll be the star student."

Jack liked Mrs. Bartlett but I was really glad I had John Gibbon. He made learning a changed thing. He connected it to the words that I loved. I would really, really miss him.

It made me think that now I'd have to say no to the Emily poem asking if I was nobody too. These days I felt I was somebody, somebody who learned stuff. I just remembered that I had given James that poem before I knew he wanted to disappear. That's the other thing story tellers and poem makers do. They help us name a feeling that's tricky to know. They give us these hints that turn around in our brain until it matches some feeling that we have. And it helps us to know that they had that feeling too. Emily's poem says "Don't tell." She knew how important secrets were.

I was good at waiting. From the day I got back after Christmas I was waiting to go home for good. Lots of things were happening right off, so it didn't seem so much like waiting. First, there was the day of a new year, and then my birthday, and then Jack's leaving day.

It was not only a new year, but a new decade, and the start of the second half of the century. A decade is counting the years by ten, and now we were up to fifty, 1950. Half way into the twentieth century. At first it seemed confusing that 1950 would be called the twentieth century. But then I realized it was just like when I reach my seventh birthday, I'll begin my eighth year counting the time that I'm living through, my eighth winter and my eighth summer, instead of the time that's past.

———————

realize

/ˈrē(ə)ˌlīz/

verb

1. become fully aware of something as a fact; understand clearly.

2. cause something desired or anticipated to happen.

We got to celebrate the new year with hats and horns and popcorn, but not at midnight. We said happy new year at nine o'clock before we had to be in bed with lights out. But the sounds of the city woke me up at midnight. People were blowing their car horns and I could hear voices from somewhere, shouting and singing. I went to my window and

I saw fireworks. At least I think they were fireworks. They were pretty far away and I had never seen fireworks before.

"Happy New Year," I said. I just whispered it, but it was a nice hello to the new decade.

The next day was my birthday. We had cupcakes at dinner and mine had a candle and everybody sang. That day at tutoring John Gibbon had given me a nice paper map of the whole world. After dinner, Nurse Hale helped me tape it on the wall in my room. The globe, of course, was the real shape of the world spinning in space. But the map helped me learn all the continents and oceans and countries. The world was big, really big.

The kind of sad thing that day in tutoring was I realized that David could hardly read. David and I took turns working with John and then working on our own. Usually I went to a corner behind a shelf of books, but that day I had to spread out these number cards on the other table. I had to match the products that were the same, like four times four is sixteen and two times eight is sixteen. Anyhow, I heard David trying to read and how he couldn't sound out the words. He wasn't getting the prize of reading which was the idea that landed in you, sometimes with a thud that surprised you with a laugh or a scary feeling or a sad tingle in the back of your neck. I realized that the sounds had to move fast to get that prize.

Realize was my new favorite word. Lots of words had different meanings, but realize had two meanings that connected to my waiting to go home. The first meaning, "being clearly aware, seeing something true for the first time" joined the "make something happen" meaning, like realizing a dream. The clearer things became, the more I could make them happen. John Gibbon liked that idea when I told him.

Part of my homework each day was to write down ideas about topics, to be the writer for someone else's reading. I had different topics each week. This week it was birds and I had a neat book with bird pictures to help me.

Jack's discharge at the end of the month was more mixed-up feelings in me, stirring together a dark and light that made the approaching days grey. Jack was the most excited, and the most absolutely sure that he was ready to get out of anybody that was discharged. So I made sure to only be excited for him and really hide my sad part. Jack's aunt had stayed in a hotel that whole month so she could visit him every Saturday, and they had meetings together twice a week with his doctor and Mrs. Bencloski. There was an uncle that his Aunt Marta was married to that fished and swam. Their boy was a cousin a few years younger than Jack that he liked, and altogether they were a family.

It turned out that Jack's new town was actually a city, Annapolis, in a different state, Maryland, with a big bay, Chesapeake. I showed Jack these things on a map and we both got excited.

The morning of his discharge, I saw Jack in the game room and I said, "What's crackin', Jack?" We both laughed.

After he left, I told a little lie to Nurse Higgins that I needed to go to my room because I didn't feel good. I lay on my bed and cried. There was a large sadness that spread out over people that maybe you didn't even know and you would never know and it repeated its ways in different lives and it made my sadness look small. I was truly happy for Jack and I realized feelings could have completely opposite names, confusing and deep inside me. There I go, realizing again. No wonder it's my favorite word these days.

Of all the kids that were here when I first came to Western, only Arnie was still here. Kids left and kids came. There were fifteen kids on the floor now. I was still the youngest. I told new kids about how things worked here, you know, with the cafeteria and laundry and lights out. I also told them about swimming and movies and fun things that would be coming up.

But the truth is I was waiting. Waiting to go home for good. It wasn't until Saint Patrick's Day, that day with lots of green stuff, that I actually had my discharge date, April 1st. I told Dr. Brenaman that I hoped I wasn't going to get April-fooled about going home, and you know what? He laughed.

That week spring came. It was my eighth spring and I could follow the longer light into my eighth summer. Joanne was my Saturday visitor. She told me that Daddy Ray was drinking again, but Mom wouldn't tell anyone at Western so it wouldn't change my going home for good.

"I wanted you to know because, well, he just started and he'll probably be still drinking when you get home."

"Is Mom mad and yelling and stuff?"

"I'm not there but Maria tells me it's not like it used to be. Mom just takes over business things more and Dad drinks and sleeps it off and drinks and after two or three weeks, he goes to Bethel's to get sober. It's crazy but what are you going to do?"

Joanne's question meant what can anybody do, not just me. And really it meant there's nothing you can do.

"It'll work out, Billy. So what have you been learning in tutoring?"

"Well the spring that just happened is really called the vernal equinox and the daylight in our part of the world is equal and starts to get more and more daylight until summer. But Mr. Gibbon explained that the Earth doesn't change its tilt, like I thought, it's just that the rays of the sun come straight at us as we orbit around it and at some points, well, I still get it mixed up."

"Me too," Joanne said.

"This is my last visitor's day."

"That's right. I didn't think of that. Next Saturday you'll be going home."

"I'm a little bit nervous."

"Sure, that's natural. I think I'll drive home on Friday and Mom and I will pick you up on the 1st. She doesn't like driving that far. I'll give her a call tonight."

"I'll miss visiting with just you and me like we do sometimes."

"You know what I'll do? Some weekend, I'll pick you up and we'll drive to Grove City and you can stay at my apartment for the whole weekend."

"That will be fun. Is Grove City a big city?"

"No. In fact it's just a town but you'll like it."

When Joanne left, I didn't feel sad because I knew I'd be seeing her and everyone real soon. I was really glad that Mom wouldn't tell anyone at Western about Daddy Ray drinking. My knowing about it became a secret, and my silence in another way became a lie. It made me think about how certain kinds of secrets were silent lies.

That week, coming back from swimming, I noticed the big sign at the top of the building, Western Psychiatric Hospital. These final weeks had made me think about the beginning and how everything was strange and new. Of course the opposite of the new that I felt now, wasn't old. I couldn't name that feeling. I've been here for a little over eight months except for three days at Christmas. And now that start was at an end. My first year in school had a start and an end with its passing and stuff. But school was only during the day and not on weekends. Psychiatric was an always thing with locked doors and the end was actually the beginning. No wonder I felt confused and kind of scared in those last days. But I never mentioned that to Dr. Brenaman. I talked about how I was looking forward to my new school.

John Gibbon hung up the phone and placed it on top of one of the stacks of papers on his dining room table. That stack was notes and pages of his Master's dissertation: *Outliers in the Learning Curve*.

He had stretched the phone cord as far away from the baby's room as he could. If his nine week old son slept the whole time while his wife was at her morning class, he could finish the final paperwork and phone calls that would facilitate William Calvin's transition from his tutorial to the classroom. He had tutored Billy for almost seven months. Because the state mandated a standardized system for testing progress, he was acutely aware of the huge incremental changes that had occurred in that time. Billy's obsession with words, their nuances, multiple meanings and opposites had sharpened a focus on his own love of words. In his conversations that morning with Dr. Brenaman and Connie Bencloski he had been careful to avoid using any psychological terms or references. It had required a conscious effort in his final report as well. Throughout he had been reminded that his role and his assessment had to be strictly academic. But he intuitively believed that Billy Calvin's growing self-esteem as a learner couldn't be separated from his psychological profile.

---

teach
/tēCH/

verb
show or explain to someone how to do something.

learn
/lərn/

verb
gain or acquire knowledge of or skill in something by study, experience, or being taught.

It was in that first week when Billy asked if John could learn him the states on the map that John's correction had started a running dialogue about the words teach and learn. Were they opposites? Well, sort of but not really. Billy was never satisfied with the categorical language of the dictionary. The naming of feelings that he saw as his main task of therapy made him stretch words into his own personal experience, nuanced and sometimes contradictory.

John Gibbon learned to do this himself, especially in the months that he anticipated fatherhood and in the first days of holding his infant son. In attaching words to these experiences he had learned from Billy Calvin, and in that learning had come to love him. This interchange of their roles, to teach, to learn, connected them both for the rest of their lives.

He grabbed at the ringing phone to avoid waking the baby.

"Good morning. This is Sister Mary Michael."

"Thank you for getting back to me, Sister."

"William Calvin has been assigned to my third grade class. I can see from the test scores in the packet that you sent me that he's a very high level achiever."

"Yes. He's also very creative and very well behaved."

"Of course that's under very different conditions. I do have concerns about how he will adjust to a classroom setting."

"There certainly will be an adjustment period as he integrates into a classroom, but I'm confident that it will be a smooth transition."

"Let me be forthright. Do you think the child still poses any danger?"

John Gibbon almost laughed at the use of the word danger. "Absolutely not," he said. That line of inquiry should have been referred to Dr. Brenaman, but John wanted to stop it immediately. "It's been determined that the shooting incident was an accident," he said. This was really going out on a limb. The only substantiation he had of that was Dr. Helen Logan's report that generally contradicted Dr. Brenaman's diagnosis.

"Well, there are concerns." Sister Mary Michael hesitated. "Of course we want to accommodate the child and the family, but there are concerns."

"I think, Sister, if you just regard Billy as you would any other new student you will find that he'll be an asset to your third grade."

"I'll do that Mr. Gibbon."

"Please feel free to call in the coming weeks if you have any questions."

"Thank you. Have a good day."

---

concern

/kən'sərn/

verb

1. relate to; be about.

2. worry someone; make anxious.

When John checked the baby's room, he found the infant wide awake. The baby's smile broke into a laugh when he saw his father. John couldn't resist picking him up, walking him from room to room in the tiny apartment. Concern, the verb, and concerns, the plural noun, played in his mind. He would have to put a professional check on his own concern for Billy Calvin whom he would never see again after next week.

I kept my silent lie about Daddy Ray drinking and told that other lie about looking forward. The truth was, I was looking backward to when the *in* and *out* signs first appeared. I never talked about the different words that appeared like signs at the edge of my vision. I told John Gibbon about it in a hinting way once and he said it was called peripheral vision. I looked the word up in my dictionary but I couldn't always remember it or pronounce it so I didn't like it much. I sometimes wondered how many of my secrets were lies.

CHAPTER 25

Going Home

THAT FINAL WEEK, the chimes from the nearby clock tower began to wake me during the night. I had stopped hearing them altogether for months, but now they seemed loud. I was counting time, the passing hours and days, and every proof of it caught my notice.

I awoke with a dream trapped in my remembering. It was the exact dream I had before, a long time ago. I had forgotten about that little blue shovel that went with my bucket. There is a war on in this dream and it's loud. Most of the dream is just digging and digging with my little blue shovel into a safe place on the hill. And then the shovel is a knife and I stab at a someone coming at me and my hand is covered in blood like Daddy Ray's is in the slaughterhouse and then the chimes wake me. They sound six times but there's still no morning light. I go to the window and look out as if I could see the tower where the sound is coming from. I've never even figured out where it is. The room is too dark to see my clock, so I can't know the hour until the chimes stop. It's a truer thing about time, knowing it only when it changes into past. It's Monday morning and these are my last days in psychiatric. I lay back down but I can't fall back to sleep. Dreams are always my secret. Once in a while Dr. Brenaman asks me if I can remember what I've dreamt, and I always say no even though I sometimes can. I never sleep in my dreams. I wander, never stopping, through places I've never seen. One dream I remembered, I was lost and all the places I walked through were strange and kind of scary and then I could hear singing far away just soft and when it got louder I was crossing the bridge at Allen Creek.

That day in tutoring, Mr. Gibbon showed me and David a movie about the parts of the body; brain, heart, muscles, skin. I couldn't remember them all when it was over. But David did. He was smart when he didn't need to read, so John was teaching him without reading until he learned better.

John scheduled my last three days of tutoring by myself. He said we needed to go over my final Pennsylvania tests and talk about my new school, and wrap up lessons in each subject. I liked that wrap up saying, like the lessons were a gift.

"The movie yesterday about the parts of the body was good," I said.

"How many can you remember?"

"Let me see. Skin, bones, muscles, brain, heart, lungs, skin. I said that one."

"Good recall," John said. "The organs are each part of a system. They are made up of tissues and the tissues are made up of cells. For now, I just wanted you to get the general idea of how the body works inside."

"The stomach. That's another one."

"Yes."

"What's the opposite of part?" I asked.

"What do you think?"

"The whole thing?"

"And what's the whole thing in our lesson?"

"The body?"

"Yes. I'll name some parts, and you try to guess the whole thing."

"Okay."

"Pedals, handlebars, wheels."

"Bicycle."

"Good. Roof, door, window, staircase."

"A house."

"Alright. Petal, stem, leaf."

"A flower."

"Good."

"It's like everything is a part or a whole and is really both," I said. "Like with teaching and learning. The part and the whole are two sides of a naming just like teach and learn are two sides of a naming. Sort of opposite but more like one is inside of the other and it's there always with the knowing."

"Always," John said. There were tears in his eyes although he was smiling big.

Goodbyes make you feel funny, even when you really want to go. John Gibbon was on Thursday because there is no tutoring on Friday. I turned in my lesson books but he said I could keep my dictionary, and he gave me the bird book that I used in my writing lesson a few weeks ago. I picked up my final clay thing that was finished in the kiln from occupational therapy. It was chess pieces in black and white. I made it from a mold and it came out nice. Dr. Brenaman shook my hand after our last meeting. David and some of the other guys thanked me. I'm not sure what for. Arnie said, "Goodbye, Billy." That was only the second time I ever heard him talk. I didn't think he even knew my name. I hugged him and he smiled. When Bonnie Mom and Joanne picked me up Saturday morning the nurses hugged me, and Tom knuckle rubbed my head.

I was going home. I had waited and now I wasn't waiting. I was excited about seeing everybody and just being in my house and my room. But it also meant I could be alone in my favorite places.

I stared out the back window as we drove down Darragh Hill. I watched the sign at the top of the building disappear. It did say hospital after the words Western Psychiatric. If I was sick, am I cured now? I needed to be alone. The wide world was in me now. All my knowing and words were held tight inside to help me know how I know.

The first days home were too much fussing. I would start school next week and I really wanted to go out and be by myself. Daddy Ray was home and wasn't drinking but he seemed louder and different. The good thing is, he was playing the piano and singing again. Some of the songs I knew, but there were some new ones that were just now hits, which means a lot of people like them. My favorites were 'Chattanooga Choo Choo' and 'Music, Music, Music'. I sat on the bench beside him and he would tap me on the chest when he started with "Pardon me boy," and everyone would laugh. He held my hand and made my finger play 'Heart and Soul' and his left hand played the other part. Eleanor played 'My Darling Clementine' and Daddy Ray stood at the window, his back to us and sang, his voice full and true and everyone was quiet.

After a few days I was allowed to walk alone to the upper field by the stream where you couldn't see any houses, not even ours. I had named it Earth and I still felt that connection to the sky and ground, the smell of the air and the smell of the dirt. It wasn't really a secret place anymore, because I had told James and John Gibbon and secrets disappear when they're told.

I found a miniature bridge I had built across the stream although most of the little roads had been washed away. For the first time I followed the stream flowing beside the slate piles behind our slaughterhouse clear down to Allen Creek. I pretended to see it, running still into the Monongahela River joining the Allegheny to become the Ohio and then the Mississippi, into the Gulf of Mexico. At first they were just map words but John Gibbon made me follow the blue with my finger and said it was over two thousand miles to its end. I touched my hand into the little stream, knowing, it became the after and after, real paths of water.

Going back home, I crossed through the lower meadow. It was muddy now. Not like in the warm days, when the buttercups had blossomed and I would lie quiet and the rabbits would come real close to eat and eat and they would listen at me with their ears. If I stirred they stopped and became statue-still. They seemed to be pretending an invisibility and they were calm inside that pretend. It made me remember how calm that could be.

I had to go back to school, but I had weekends and warmer days and growing light to be out and alone. I had a lot of wondering to piece together. It would take a long time.

My teacher, Sister Mary Michael, had lots of rules, but I followed them and she was nice when you followed her rules. John Gibbon's ways of learning had made me a good student. I finished the year with good grades and guess what? Excellent deportment.

I avoided the playground by walking along the railroad tracks until I came to the Red and White store which wasn't red or white. I went there and to the post office sometimes. I didn't run into kids I knew. None of the kids from our town went to Saint Edwards School. Adults were polite but not friendly. One day near the end of the school year, I ran into Cappy at the post office. I said hey, and he did too. I got our mail which was just an electric bill that I stuffed in my pocket.

When Cappy and I got outside he looked at me and smiled.

"I'll be a sonofabitch if it isn't Billy Calvin. Killer Calvin. I heard you were in jail."

"Yeah, but the governor pardoned me. They can do that. How's school going?"

"It's all over. She flunked me. I gotta do it all over again. I could have used you, Calvin. The good news is Miss Parsons is getting married and moving to Detroit."

"That's a break. Maybe now she won't be so mad about the Miss or Mrs. thing."

Cappy kept walking with me. We walked through the playground which was empty. He walked me up to the top of Tipple Road. We sat on the one side looking down into the creek.

"I go to a different school now. We're not out for another three weeks."

"Were you really in jail?"

"Nah, just away for a while with my sister, Joanne. She has an apartment in Grove City."

"So I guess you weren't lying about that rifle."

"I never lied back then. I do now, though."

"Hell, Calvin, you were always smart but now you're a smart-ass too." Cappy gave me a pat on the back. "I gotta get going."

"Good to see you Cappy." I watched him walk back down the hill and out of sight. Nine months had passed since I had seen him last. The time it takes to be born. Ha. Cappy wouldn't be my sometimes-friend anymore. He wasn't really a friend like James or Jack who I'd never see again but would stay as always friends.

Seeing Cappy again gave me another realize. I mean another way of realizing something. Things happen that change me and I can never predict it or even know if it's good or bad when it's happening.

---

predict

/pre dikt/

verb

say or estimate that something will happen in the future or will be a consequence of something.

School finally came to an end. It was good. Not like tutoring with John Gibbon, but I learned stuff and I liked learning. That next week it was the summer solstice and I went to my very favorite place, the abandoned coke ovens, especially the one with the hole in the top that created a beam of light. I sat in the far corner and watched the beam brighten as the sun moved overhead. I had shown it to Maria, so it wasn't secret, but it was special. Maybe because it was a thing that had one purpose when it was built, but now was changed into this wonderful place because of the way it was broken.

●

The decaying coke oven was like a cathedral to Billy Calvin whose whole sense of the sacred, a word he didn't know then, focused clearly in the solitary time that he sat in the corner watching the beam of light pass through the missing bricks in the dome. This is where we leave him. Somehow in the old man's mind his boy story ends here. Of course there are stories that connect to that small smiling boy sitting in the corner of the abandoned coke oven in the dinosaur town where he grew up, but they are not this story. This is a story about words. The coming to words of the baby, the boy. The losing of words of the old man staring into the fire. It's the story a baby could tell, if he had the words to tell it. The story an old man could tell if the right words haven't already disappeared.

There is an event that happened that night, the night of the summer solstice and the start of Billy Calvin's eighth summer. Event is a construct built by one person's memory and this one was kept alive and true by Bill Calvin into his old age. He and Eleanor had gone out into the front yard to lay on the grass and look at the starry night. It was warm and cloudless. They had been allowed to stay up later until the night was completely dark. Joanne had been visiting. She and Lena came out and laid beside them. Bonnie Calvin turned out the house lights and the porch light and Carolyn and Maria came out and joined the group. Ray Calvin went down and turned off the lights by the shop and even the light that lit the Calvin Provision sign on the top of the slaughterhouse. Then he and his wife went and laid on the grass beside their six children. The total darkness enveloped them as they lay there in silence, the billions of stars glittering from unfathomable distances. Billy broke the silence when he spoke.

"Here we are on Earth," he said.

CHAPTER 26

Now Again

RUTHIE WAS RIGHT. Tutoring again focused my days. We extended the schedule, meeting in the little room at Jefferson Library on Monday, Wednesday and Friday. My sense of time plugged into this pattern immediately. The "queens", as I began to think of them, were charming. Queen Christina the Third admitted in a piece of writing how much she hated school and I told her I hated school when I was her age. Christina the Fourth was the eager student. She didn't really need me, but she loved the group and I loved letting her boast her considerable creative talent. Captain Johnny remained cautious, reticent. He kept secret the world he lived in, slowly revealing a fiercely intelligent mind.

———

reticent
/ˈredəsənt/

adjective
not revealing one's thoughts or feelings readily.

During my early years of teaching, I was at my best with the reticent student. In my latter years, that kind of student mostly disappeared. The gentle nudging, the watchful eye needed to spot the spark of engagement and use it to ignite a curiosity, became obsolete skills. Through my final teaching years, most of the fifth grade students I had were constantly jockeying to answer the question, to present their writing, to be the focus of attention. Their games didn't require waiting for their turn, and they had little interest in what their classmates wrote or had to say in a discussion.

I set up a random name selection program for my Smart Board. It beeped and flashed before landing on a student name. I could move through different lessons without calling on the same student twice. The kids loved it. It made their competition for my attention fair. I worked hard at teaching and I loved it. But in the end it was enervating. My classroom on the fourth floor looked out on Leroy Street in Greenwich Village with a direct view of the Hudson River as it flowed its final mile. Oddly, it also had an angled view of the Empire State Building, sparkling in the morning sun. As the years passed, I became acutely aware of the fast paced information world I was keeping out each day that I closed my classroom door and began the morning lessons.

With tutoring groups, usually three students, that need, to show, to tell, to answer was easily satisfied. But then, there he was, Captain Johnny, the reticent student.

The mid-nineteenth century origin of the word reticent joined the Latin, *re*, meaning expressing intensive force with the verb, *tacere*, to be silent. It identified the driving energy of my own childhood, an intense force toward silence.

It was an odd time to be looking at vocabulary and written expression with the Queens Christina and Captain Johnny. Odd to be grappling with ways to expand their vocabulary as mine diminished. They were gentle with my forgetting. They nudged me into recalling what I wanted to say. But as the weeks passed, the panic increased with each incident.

Once during lessons, I lost a common New York word, and made the mistake of describing and miming it. It was Johnny who gave me the word.

"I was late today, so I grabbed a . . . you know, you put up your hand in the street, you hail it." I raised an open hand in the air.

"Taxi," Johnny said. He switched from his usual downward gaze and stared into my eyes in direct unsettling concern.

The girls thought I was joking. We regularly did a writing exercise in which we defined common words: pencil, smile or roof, explaining them to a fictional Martian who never heard of such a thing. I laughed when the girls laughed but Johnny didn't.

I felt that Johnny understood my secret of forgetting and that magnified my panic.

I finished up the lesson as I always did by briefly reviewing the assignment sheet for our next meeting. "Now this assignment is a made-up story, none of it has to be true. Do you remember what we call that?"

"Fiction," Queen Christina the Third said.

"That's right."

"What's a novel, Mr. Calvin?" Christina the Fourth said.

"*Harry Potter*'s a novel, and *Shiloh*," Johnny said.

"Yes, novels are long fictional stories," I said.

"But *Shiloh* is true," Johnny said.

"No, it's realistic. Unlike the Harry Potter novels, it could happen. But it's still made up. Do you all see the difference? Let's try to write a full page for Monday. And this time keep your story realistic. It didn't happen but it could happen. The only starter is the word *if*."

"Just *if*?" Christina the Third said.

"Yes, your majesty, just *if*. If was one of my favorite words when I was your age. Do any of you have favorite words?" They all shook their heads silently. "Well each of your stories has to start with if. Let's go, your parents are waiting."

"My babysitter's picking me up today," Christina the Fourth said. "Now that's one of my least favorite words, babysitter."

"You could change it to studentsitter or queensitter."

"See you Monday, Mr. Calvin."

I let them go at the top of the staircase. They ran. It was Friday and now school was completely out. I started home, but then without thinking I went west toward the river. My mind was flooded with the emotion of losing the word taxi and the recognition of Johnny's concern. In the short time of tutoring Johnny Norkus, the silence of his reticence had anchored something identifiable in the self I experienced at his age.

———

identify
/ī'den(t)ə‚fī/

verb
establish or indicate who or what someone or something is.

In that way he was an asset to this grappling. He gave me a handle on my own very different childhood by some shared notion of silence.

I walked west on 10th Street to Hudson Avenue. Crossed to Christopher Street and continued west toward the Hudson River. Countless taxies passed me and I said the word as I saw each one; Taxi. Taxi. Taxi. How could I be losing this simple naming of the world. Words were everything to me. They were the links to how I connect to, I don't know, maybe just how I connect, period. That's the fear, if I can't give words to a narrative, can I be what? Awake? Me? Oh where have you gone Billy Boy, Billy Boy? Where have you gone charming Billy?

Our waking days are so clearly a narrative, an imperative, a declarative, an interrogative. It's a mystery how we invoke the words to form the anecdote, the explanation, the question, the story.

———

invoke
/in'vōk/

verb
to put into effect or operation, to implement.

My walking felt so aimless, so dreamlike, that when I found myself walking up the steps to Saint Veronica's, it didn't surprise me. The Catholic church on Christopher Street was built over a hundred years ago. I had been there numerous times for memorial services during the early years of the AIDS epidemic. The span between those services reduced to weeks. So many dead that living, not being infected, for a gay man in New York City became framed with an odd guilt. I had seen, but had forgotten about, a plaque in the vestibule of the church with the names of those who died and were memorialized here. I read each name. Only a few jogged my memory.

Dan and I had moved to New York, to the apartment where I still live, in 1980. Not long after that a friend, a doctor who I knew in Washington, Pennsylvania where I first taught, sent us a small brochure. It was the CDC's morbidity and mortality report. I still have it filed somewhere. It cited eight cases of Kaposi's Sarcoma in otherwise healthy homosexual men. Dan and I did not become infected. A graph of deaths in New York City during those years, has intervals separated by a thousand. It climbed as the decade passed, two thousand, three, four, leveling at nine thousand before it begins to decline and our being alive becomes less of an anomaly.

We lived many decades of contentment after that. He was my great love, my calming love, my laughing love. We had codes of silliness that kept us both on course. We were able to marry a few years before he died. The Supreme Court cited "changing norms" in the majority opinion. "You best be changing your norm," he would say.

Even in the difficult year after Dan's death of cardiac arrest, "the graceful exit" he would have called it, I felt a completion, a contentment, about our decades together. As my own life stretches out from that point, there is a loneliness, but it does not interrupt the contentment. So it's odd that this losing of words has introduced this rend, this rip in the fabric of that contentment.

It's rooted somehow in the very earliest coming to words. My earliest confusion of words included the word dead. That first confusion courted an inexorable fear. It wasn't a fear of dying, but a fear of killing. That I would have to go to war, that I would have to kill. Men kill. Boys become men.

Because of my time in Western Psychiatric, I never did go to war. But

I did witness that kind of killing on a sunny September day in 2001 when nearly 3,000 people were killed. The principal came to each classroom door, called us into the hall, whispers; there had been an accident involving a plane crashing into the World Trade Center. We were to say nothing to the students until further notice. My class was scheduled for art. I dropped them off and ran out the Bleecker Street entrance, crossing east to Sixth Avenue. I could see the North Tower in flames. The streets were crowded. I heard the truth spoken out loud all around me: No accident. Both towers, The Pentagon. Another plane down in Pennsylvania. Dan was in the adjacent Deutsche Bank building. I ran back up the block to the school. The South Tower had collapsed. We all were evacuated to the basement cafeteria. We still were not telling the children. We waited. Passed out board games. Waited. Students were released to parents intermittently throughout the day. We waited into the early afternoon. Finally, I received a note from the office: five words scrawled on a message pad: "Dan is safe, back home." I still have that note. Although the school community had many family members in the towers, all were evacuated safely. I stayed with my students until they were all picked up. It was dark by the time I was walking home. The smoky stench filled the air.

I never knew and so I'll never know if my father killed during World War II. The slaughterhouse, watching my father butchering the animals, made all that confusion tangible. The stuff of baby dreams. I lost touch with my father after he and Bonnie Mom divorced. Or I should say he lost touch with me. With all of us. He went away.

---

away

/əˈwā/

adverb

to or at a distance from a particular place, person, or thing.

I guess he never looked back, so maybe we just disappeared.
When Bonnie Mom was at the end of her life, she didn't recognize

us when we visited. Not at first. Then the timbre of our voice, our name, our motion would spark a connection. "It's Lena, Mom" or "Hi, Mom, its Eleanor here." "Hey sweetie, how you doing? It's Bill."

"Ah, Billy," she would say. The name connected to the person before it faded again and required reminding, often in the same visit. She had round-the-clock care and so she stayed in the house where we grew up. I have this memory. I am visiting from New York about a month before she died. We are sitting together facing the windows. The early warmth has allowed us to open the windows. She speaks very little and so we sit in silence looking out over the back fields, enjoying the light breeze. Carolyn comes in behind us. She has just arrived from Columbus, Ohio where she lives. She touches my mother's shoulder and leans in to kiss her on the cheek.

"Carolyn, what a wonderful surprise," my mother says.

"Yes, how did you know?" Carolyn crosses to me and we hug.

"Wind Song by Prince Matchabelli," my mother says.

"Yes, I've had it for ages. I ration it out for special occasions." She pulls a chair close to our mother and cups one of her hands in both of hers. "Occasions like this one," Carolyn says.

"Prince George Matchabelli was an amateur chemist," my mother says. "A Georgian prince and an ambassador to Italy. He fled the Soviet Union and emigrated to the United States after the Russian revolution. His wife was an actress, not famous though. They started the perfume line out of an antique shop they ran in New York City."

Carolyn and I looked at each other and both shrugged at exactly the same time which made us laugh. I move to my mother and kiss her on both cheeks. It was the last time I saw her.

The towering openness of Saint Veronica's where I was sitting in the back pew, for I don't know how long, disappeared into a claustrophobia and I left abruptly, continuing toward the Hudson River. I walked out on to one of the piers now renovated into a beautiful park setting. I sat on a bench facing the splendor of the setting sun. I watched the Statue of Liberty moving from gleaming light to shadow and I cried, a bawling, blustery cry, the so-called good cry. For all the words lost and all the words better served by those wordless tears.

There is a halting confusion to the way we sort the world that stays in our bones and sets the direction of our life. If and if and if, an always favorite word.

As I begin to walk home, the city lights are coming on. It's dark by the time I get to my apartment and I make a fire in the fireplace in spite of the fact that the night air is only beginning to chill. I put the kettle on for tea. If I lose the words for kettle and tea will I still be able to do this? There is a word I gave to an idea or maybe a feeling when I was a child. The word was *wide* and I've held it in my mind as a touchstone to something I can only understand in a hinting way. I always thought I would rename this idea and lately I've found it. It's become my new favorite word. I open the A through O volume of the Oxford English dictionary. I need the magnifying glass to read the words. I love the thinness of the pages, the sheer volume of listed words. I've known the word I'm looking for but I want to see it. I find it: *ineffable*.

––––––––––

ineffable
/inˈefəb(ə)l/

adjective
too great or extreme to be expressed or described in words.

The old man sits by the fire. There is a chill. He invites you to take the comfortable chair, closest to the blazing logs. The sparks bounce off the fine meshed screen. He takes a grey throw and covers your lap. "A story is the words between the remembering," he says. "It is the connections we invent to make it comprehensible." He sits back down in the rocker and begins: "Once upon a time." You laugh. He begins again. "It was and was not so."

Acknowledgments

I WISH to acknowledge readers of the early chapters: Those participating in workshops at *Writers and Books* and *Night Writers*. My thanks to the readers of the completed novel: Dianne Shawley, Rosemarie McErlain-Cassidy, Rebecca Boivin and especially the many hours throughout by Cheryl Tiffany and Bob Calabrese. Thanks to my Editors: Jim Madden and Doris Walsh and to Anne Kilgore for the book design.

Discussion Questions

1. An infant develops the ability to speak in the language he/she hears. How does that extend to the variation of the words he/she learns? Think of Billy Calvin's fascination with the word *borrow* or his confusion with the word *grades*.

2. We hear the story narrated by Billy Calvin beginning when he is two and a half years old. He loves words and especially being read to. What very early stories do you remember as a child?

3. Billy is the only boy in a family of six children. How does gender play a role in the narrative of the novel?

4. The story takes place before television. What words from the radio programs that Billy heard were important to him?

5. Billy's friend from the playground, Cappy McLaughlin, uses swear words constantly. How did these words become Cappy's favorite words?

6. The language in the Calvin household is monitored. We learn that *stupid*, and *fat* were not nice to say. How does being nice become a part of behaving for Billy?

7. What rules do you remember about behavior from your childhood? At what age were you when these rules were imposed?

8. The novel includes dictionary entries for simple words that we all know. How does this affect the narrative? In what ways does the author lead us to reconsider these words?

9. Bill Calvin, as an old man, narrates, "I will have to depend on the omniscient lies of this fiction to parse out the few available truths." What does omniscient mean? Why does the narrator call them lies?

10. The varied voices of fiction change between first person narration by Billy Calvin, and two omniscient narrations: the events Billy Calvin couldn't know about and the events of Billy Calvin as an old man. What information and understanding does the reader get from these different voices?

11. "The old man sits by the fire" sequences revert to the archetype of the old man. How does that differ from Bill Calvin as an old man in the present day?

12. Paramnesia, the distortion of memory in which fact and fantasy are confused, is one of the first words defined in the novel. How does that set up the narrative conceits that the novel takes on?

13. *Dead* is the most confusing word to the toddler, Billy Calvin. How does he come to know that word and what things that follow in the novel contribute to that confusion?

14. How does the world of the family that Billy experiences, and his rules for behaving, compare with the rules of school and the rules of law?

15. After the rifle incident, Billy is placed in Western Psychiatric Institution. How does this mental hospital differ from other portraits of mental hospitals in fiction?

16. Billy describes the hospital world as "wide" and the extreme emotional experiences with other patients as "wide". What does he mean by this and what word does he finally equate with wide?

17. Billy explains that everything at Western Psychiatric is a therapy. How does this idea become a major theme in the novel?

18. *Teach* and *learn* and *part* and *whole* are defined words in the novel. How are these words also primary themes?

19. What would you say are some of your own favorite words?

20. *If* is a defined word that is key in the story telling. What part does that word play? How does the word *if* figure in your own life?

21. The question words: who, what, when, where, why and how, are parsed through by Billy Calvin as a child and as an old man. How does ones understanding of these words effect the understanding of things in general?

22. What does the psychological term "repression" mean? Do you think repression demands uncovering for a healthy mental life?

23. In what way does the dysfunction of the Calvin family influence the legal and social services response to Billy Calvin? How different is contemporary intervention in dysfunctional families? What are the consequences if they get it wrong?

About the Author

BILL CASTLE is a teacher and playwright. His off-Broadway productions include: *The Diaries of Trudy Sagebrush, Keep the Change, Talking in the Rain* and *Slow Dancing in the Fast Lane*. In addition, he has performed his work in New York City at Re Cher Chez, The Kitchen, Franklin Furnace and Folk City. He taught fifth grade at Our Lady of Pompeii School in Greenwich Village before retiring. His plays for children, produced at the school, include *The Chance of Change* and *Time Storm*. He is a graduate of Penn State University and did graduate studies at Penn State and the University of Pittsburgh. He currently resides in Rochester, New York. *It Was and Was Not So* is his first novel. He can be contacted at: itwasandwasnotso@gmail.com